SOUTHERN PEACH PIE AND A DEAD GUY

a Poppy Peters mystery

A. Gardner

SOUTHERN PEACH PIE AND A DEAD GUY

CHAPTER ONE

───────

My first encounter with a southern guy isn't going so well. So far I've admitted I have never tried sweet tea, and my big toe is a little too long for the shoes I am wearing. *Nice one, Poppy.* Now he is going to think I am a weird westerner with a foot fetish. I try hard not to look down at my black, high-heeled boots. *Why am I the only one on campus wearing any black?*

"My name is Cole," the man says with a grin on his face. I reach out to shake his hand. My palms are sweating just like every other place on my body. *I haven't even turned thirty yet, and I'm already having hot flashes.* It is going to take me some time to get used to this heat.

"Poppy Peters," I reply. I wipe my forehead and underneath my eyes. I bite my lip when I see a bit of smeared mascara on the side of my finger. It is so humid my makeup is melting off. "Is it always this hot here?"

"Welcome to Georgia." Cole chuckles and shrugs as we walk towards the student bakery. Cole is one of the first students I bumped into at the registration office. His lemon-colored T-shirt shines bright compared to his dark skin, and his impressive physique makes me look at him twice. His eyes are intriguing— an even mix of blue and green.

As we walk, I can't help but admire how lush the vegetation is on campus. Every tree outstretches towards the sidewalks, providing a much needed break from the glaring sun. The patches of grass remind me of ocean waves, if the ocean sparkled like emeralds. Even the flowerbeds near the Administration building had bundles of purple and orange wildflowers that couldn't be contained.

"What's that smell?" I ask. "And don't say it smells like *fresh meat*. I heard a teacher in the Registrar's Office use that joke about a hundred times."

"I'll show you."

I follow Cole across campus until the heavenly smell of baked bread and sugary doughnuts grows stronger. I long for that smell sometimes. It takes me back to my schoolgirl days when I spent my weekends in the kitchen with Grandma Liz. My Grandma Liz came to Calle Pastry Academy when she was in her early twenties. I imagine her tiny frame and long, dancer legs. It's a miracle that she came to this school and still stayed so thin.

"Whoa," I blurt out. My eyes widen when we come to a historic-looking building with brown-orangey bricks and tall windows that line up across the front. Through the glass I see a bustling bakery with a long line of students and campus visitors extending through the front doors and outside onto the sidewalk. I join Cole at the back of the line and discreetly adjust my black top and dark blue leggings. A serious change in wardrobe is in order if I plan on staying here.

When I was in high school, Mom always told me that I wore too much black. Ballerinas like me were supposed to be *light and dainty*, like an airy piece of sponge cake with non-fat whipped cream (no more than a dollop). Although I was one of the top dancers in my grade, I guess I looked too much like a slice of chocolate torte.

"This is the student bakery," Cole says. "We'll all be working here as part of our culinary training. A friend of mine came here a couple years ago. He told me all about it." He lifts his chin and speaks more formally than I'm used to.

"No kidding."

"Uh-huh." He keeps a grin on his face, and clasps his hands neatly in front of him. "The kitchen I work in back home isn't nearly as big as this one."

"And where is home?" I ask. I have him pegged for somewhere here in the South. I can hear it in his voice. Plus, he's way too polite.

"Atlanta," he answers. "Not far from here. But I grew up in Louisiana."

"Gotcha." I inhale another whiff of cooling pastries, and it makes my stomach rumble.

"What about you?" I can see him eyeing me as he pretends to look at something across the quad.

"Oh, I'm just your classic Oregonian ballerina looking for a fresh start."

"Ballerina?" he comments. "You don't look like a ballerina."

"Yep," I laugh. "That's what my over-bearing instructor Elena Povska said right before I fell on the bar and injured my back."

"Ouch."

Cole has that same look on his face that I've seen way too many times. His eyes are soft and sympathetic, and he's trying not to cringe. He's probably imagining my back cracking and me yelling on the floor in pain.

"I always hated it anyway." I grab a strand of my dark hair and look around at the rest of the student body. I stand out here. It feels like high school all over again, except my mom didn't send me off with a packed lunch of tuna on wheat, three pieces of celery, and a sugar-free breath mint. *The dancer's diet.*

"What about cooking? How do you feel about that?"

"I *love* it," I respond. "You know, my grandma came here. I always wanted to be just like her."

We move forward in line.

"Really," Cole says. "What does she do now?"

"After she graduated, she went back to Portland and opened her own bakery. My dad sold it after she passed away."

"Sorry to hear that," he replies.

"Circle of life." I brush off the subject and move on to avoid having to hold in any tears. I hate crying in public, even if it is only a little sniffle. "So are you going to be living on campus?"

"The program is so intense that I think just about everyone is."

"Right," I mutter. "Please tell me all the apartments have some wicked AC units or industrial fans or something?"

"Chill," he jokes. "You'll get used to the heat."

I laugh as we finally move indoors to the most coveted part of the line. I take a deep breath and close my eyes as I step across the threshold, enjoying the cool air against my cheeks. Cole watches me with a twisted smile.

"Do you think they'll let me stand in the freezer for a few minutes?" I say quietly.

"Newbies." Cole shakes his head. "What is the weather like in Oregon?"

"Portland is nothing like this." My eyes pop open when I smell something glorious. Something that teases my taste buds before I even see it. "I smell pie."

"The school's famous peach pie," Cole adds. "We will be learning how to make it pretty soon."

"I've never made a pie that smells like that. It…I don't even know how to describe it."

"It speaks to your soul?" he guesses.

"Soul food," I laugh. "Very funny."

We take a few steps towards the register, and I see the entire display of pastries and baked goods sitting neatly behind the glass. The rest of the bakery is smaller than I expected. There are a handful of café tables and a community board with flyers hanging on the wall. Most customers take their treats to-go. Most of the building is kitchen space. I move closer to get a better look at the assorted flavors of pies, buns, doughnuts, and Danishes. I don't see any labels. Only a chalkboard behind the counter with today's flavors written on it.

"Oh-my-gosh," I gasp, being careful not to drool all over my brand-new top. "It's like the ultimate PTA bake sale in here. I've never seen so many sugary things in one place."

"Don't kill me, but you only have a few minutes to decide what you want. It's almost our turn to order."

"How in the world am I supposed to do that?" My insides start to panic like they used to right before a curtain call.

"Well," Cole says, placing a hand on the counter. "Have you ever had a beignet?"

"Based on our initial sweet tea debate, what do you think?" My eyes jump to a pan of gooey-looking cinnamon rolls with orange icing. "What are those?"

"Buzz's rise and shine orange rolls," he answers. "The founder's son came up with the recipe."

"So many choices," I comment. I tap my heel against the tile floor and get a glance into the kitchen, as a student comes out with a pan of hot blueberry scones. My stomach churns a little as I think about putting on my chef's apron and joining in on the dough kneading and doughnut frying.

"What will you have?" Cole nudges my shoulder. I realize that I've been daydreaming the past few minutes, and now it is time for me to place my order. I'm oblivious. If I had the cash on hand I would order one of everything.

"We'll take two beignets, one of those hot blueberry scones, and an orange roll for Miss Indecisive." He pulls out his wallet and pays before I can object.

I place my hands on my hips and watch as he collects our box of baked delights.

"You forgot the coffee," I joke. I drink coffee like I drink water. It was the only way I could practice ballet ten hours a day and still stay standing. Cole hands me a napkin and the orange roll I stared at while in line. "Thanks, you're a peach."

"You're different from other women I've met here so far," he comments. He takes a bite of his beignet and quickly wipes the powdered sugar from his lips. We snag the last open café table and sit down across from each other.

"I know," I reply with a mouth full of citrus icing. *Dang, that is good.* My eyes dart to a sign pinned on the community board as I chew. It flaps in the breeze whenever someone opens the bakery door. "It's the high-heeled boots, right? They're a little too Goth for my taste, but I had to have them."

"No." He grins. "I like the boots. Keep the boots." He breaks the blueberry scone in half and hands me a piece. I see steam rising from the center and the rich, royal blue color of the blueberries inside. "How does a ballerina end up in a place like this? Aren't you guys all about working out all day and eating tofu?"

"I hate tofu," I reply. The paper on the community board waves as a breeze drifts through the front door. At first I only glance at it, but then my gaze freezes on two words that are printed in all caps. *MISSING STUDENT.* I stare at the picture on the poster of a younger looking student named Tom Fox who, according to the poster, went missing last semester. Underneath Tom's picture that was copied from his student ID there is a contact name and phone number for a woman named Brooke.

"Uh, Poppy?" Cole chuckles.

I realize that I have been studying the poster of Tom Fox instead of listening to Cole. He's staring at me curiously.

"Sorry." I tilt my head towards the community board. "Do students disappear often around here?"

"There's at least one per semester," he jokes. "But, honestly, stuff like that happens at every school, doesn't it?"

Not one this small.

"Maybe."

"Anyway," he continues. "Back to my question before you spaced out. Are you a culinary genius and you're just not telling me?"

"Okay, fine," I admit. "I've never worked in a kitchen before, but I'm a fast learner." I pause from devouring my orange roll and think back to my dancing days. I hated them. Every morning I would wake up wishing I had followed the advice that Grandma Liz gave me before she died. She told me to do what I love and the rest would all fall into place. Some of my best memories are baking with her. Grandma Liz was fearless. Anything I asked her to make she would try, and it always turned out to be amazing.

"You've at least made a pie before, right?"

"Of course I have," I answer, raising my eyebrows.

"From scratch?" he adds.

I let out a long breath.

"Define *scratch*." I bite the inside of my cheek and wait for him to tease me some more, but he doesn't. I'm too embarrassed to admit that I used store-bought dough the last time I made pie.

"Don't worry about it." He nods and continues eating his half of the blueberry scone. "I'll be your first official tutor."

"Thanks. I think I'm going to need it."

I've always had the baking bug, as Grandma called it, but all of high school I put it on the back burner to perfect pliés for my Juilliard audition. Mom said that four years there would work wonders for my career, and she was right. Until the day that all changed. After my back injury pushed me out of the dancing world, I realized I wasn't only good at *one* thing. I had a chance at a fresh start. A clean slate. I remember the look on my mom's and dad's faces when I told them I applied to go to Calle Pastry Academy like Grandma had. They thought I was joking. The sensible thing to do would be to become a professional ballet coach in Los Angeles or New York City. I love big cities, but I don't love them as much as a tray of Grandma's homemade snickerdoodles with extra cinnamon.

"Welcome to pastry school, Lil' Mama." Cole laughs.

* * *

My heart races as I knock on the door to my new apartment. When the school first opened in the early 1900's it was a restaurant and hotel. Later, when it was converted into a cooking school, the hotel portion became student dorms, and since then the campus has grown. The student apartments are a newer addition, but walking up to them still felt like walking up to my college dorm room. The apartment buildings look like the rest of the buildings on campus. They are all made of tan-colored stone with rows and rows of bright green brush surrounding the edges. Every patch of green on campus has fruit trees and budding wild flowers. Being surrounded by all this foliage reminds me of home, minus the mosquitoes the size of mini cupcakes.

A woman with strawberry blonde hair opens the door. A blast of cool air bursts onto my face along with the smell of chocolate cake. The familiar scent brings a smile to my face. I clutch the handle of my purse as I slowly walk inside.

"You must be my new roomie," I say, starting the conversation. "I'm Poppy."

"Hi, I'm Bree." She briefly nods and immediately retreats back to the kitchen. I shut the door behind me and follow her inside. "I bake when I'm nervous."

"I can see that," I mutter. I watch her finish icing a chocolate cake with rainbow sprinkles on top. The layered cake has smooth edges, and the color of it is a deep, milk chocolaty brown. "Now *that's* a chocolate cake."

"Thanks," she says quietly.

Bree's hair is perfectly curled, and it falls to her shoulders. Her cheeks are rosy, and the humidity makes her pale face look damp. She's wearing a pink sundress and a ruffled apron. She is heavier than me, but she fills out her dress better than I ever could.

As Bree nervously works on her cake, I walk around the apartment. The kitchen is small with a tiny fridge and an oven that heats up the entire living area. The tiles on the floor are a bit faded, and the walls could use a splash of color. They are all beige. I study the front room. It has a couch, a loveseat, and a TV. The carpet and furniture are all various shades of tan.

"Wow, this place is drab," I mutter out loud to myself.

I walk down a long hallway and pass a bathroom followed by two bedrooms. Bree already took the first room. Her bedspread matches the shade of pink on her dress. I walk into the neighboring bedroom. It isn't as cool as the front of the apartment, but it's better than sleeping in my car. I hope Cole was right when he said that I would get used to the heat.

I walk back to the kitchen, hoping I brought enough décor to liven up my room while I'm here. I will be eating, sleeping, and breathing pastry for the next year at least. I'll have to do something drastic about all the beige.

"Is it just me, or does this place look like a waiting room at a dentist's office?"

"Oh, you mean all the brown?" she asks.

"Yeah."

"I hate it too." She adds more rainbow sprinkles to the top of her cake and then takes a step back to admire it. "Do you want a piece?"

I rub my stomach, still full from the orange roll, beignet, and half of a blueberry scone that I ate with Cole.

"I am going to have to pass," I reply.

"You went to the student bakery, didn't you?"

"What gave it away?" I reply, clutching my bloated sides.

"Beware the baker's dozen."

I raise my eyebrows.

"You've heard of the freshmen fifteen, right?" she continues. "Think of the baker's dozen as the CPA *thirteen*."

"CPA?"

"Calle Pastry Academy," she states.

"Right, of course." I plop down on the couch to let my feet rest before I walk back to my car and haul in my duffle bag. "You're not from here, are you?"

"Nope," Bree answers. "I'm from Connecticut."

That explains the housewifey sundress.

"I'm not from here either. I drove all the way from Oregon. My first road trip since right before I spent four grueling years at Juilliard." I put my feet up on the coffee table and catch Bree looking at the spot where my boots touch the wood furniture. *Oh, no. She's a clean freak.* "So what's going on tonight? Where do students hang out around here?"

"I don't know," she huffs. She pulls a serving utensil from her purse. I try not to bust out laughing. She uses it to cut a piece of her chocolate cake. She lays the small piece on a white, porcelain plate and holds up her fork. "I'm going to bed early tonight. I want to get a good night's sleep before classes start tomorrow."

"What do you think our first day will be like?" I'm praying that I have a few days to get used to everything before we are thrown into the kitchen. Talking to Cole about past work experience made me nervous. I thought I would fit in here, but maybe I was wrong. It would take me longer than an hour to whip out a layered, chocolate cake as perfect as Bree's.

"I heard it's tough." She takes a bite of her masterpiece and looks up as she chews as if mentally critiquing her own dessert. "These first few days they usually try to weed out people who aren't cut out for the program."

"Oh," I mutter. "That must have been what happened to Tom Fox."

"Who?" Bree asks.

"Tom Fox," I repeat. "Have you heard of him? There's a missing student poster hanging in the bakery."

"I heard that one in five freshmen end up having a psychological breakdown after their unit one exam."

"I'm sure that's an exaggeration," I respond.

I push aside the doubt that is creeping through my head and think of Grandma Liz. She made it through with flying colors. I can make it through day one. No problem. I will just have to work extra hard. I'm no stranger to hard work. If anyone is going home this week, it won't be me.

CHAPTER TWO

———

Bree squeezes the handle of her whisk. She brought her own whisk to class, and I'm not surprised. The two of us got here before anyone else. Bree insisted on taking the front row counter. I am more of a back row kind of girl, but I agreed because I don't know anyone else. I watch as more and more students pick their seats for our first official class at Calle Pastry Academy, or CPA as Bree says.

Our classroom is one of many in this building. It serves as both a small lecture hall and a student kitchen. Our desks are metal counters – work stations. Underneath each counter are shelves with various cooking gear. I am pretty sure that the wide variety of baking utensils includes a *whisk*, but I think Bree is attached to the pastel pink handle on the one she brought from home.

I wave when I see Cole. He sits in the back row and casually folds his arms as he leans back on his stool to let another student past him. The noise level in the room goes down a notch when our first teacher of the day walks to the front of the classroom. He is wearing a chef's uniform, and he's carrying a kit of his own baking utensils. I feel butterflies in my stomach. We are going to cook today. My eyes go wide as I watch him set up his station. He looks younger than I expected, with brown hair and a pointy nose, but the stern look on his face reminds me of an old man sitting outside a women's fitting room at the mall.

"Good morning," he says, beginning class. He doesn't have an accent. He's not from around here. "First off, every teacher that you interact with during the course of this program will prefer to be addressed differently. You can call me *Professor* Sellers." He pauses to glance around the room and make sure that everyone heard his instructions. "Underneath your counter is a set of baking essentials. Please take them out and get ready to jump right in."

My hands fumble as I pull a set of pans, spoons, and mixing bowls from under my counter. I set them on the surface in front of me and gulp. I never thought I would be this nervous on my first day. My chest starts to pound, and I accidentally drop a bowl on the cement floor. It makes a loud banging noise that forces the entire class to look in my direction. My cheeks feel warm as I pick up the bowl and smile like it is no big deal.

I really suck at first impressions.

"Be careful now," the Professor adds. It sounds almost like a scolding. "Ah, there you are." He looks towards the door as another man walks in. The man has white hair, and he's tall and lanky. He is wearing a light khaki colored suit and a baby blue tie that matches the pen on his clipboard. "Everyone, this is the president of our school, Mr. Dixon."

The classroom is overtaken by complete silence as Mr. Dixon slowly walks to the front. A few students even gaze at him admirably as if they were in the presence of an A-List celebrity. I pretend to be just as amazed, but the truth is I don't know anything about Mr. Dixon other than he signed my acceptance letter.

"Thank you, Professor Sellers." Mr. Dixon places his hands on the cold countertop and studies our faces. "Welcome to your first day of pastry school." His voice is deep, and it has a southern twang to it. "Some of you have traveled far to be here, and some of you are in your own neck of the woods. But all of you have come for the same reasons: a love of food and an entrepreneurial appetite. So good luck y'all." He nods and looks down at his clipboard. "Francois Calle, the school's founder, emigrated all the way from France almost a hundred years ago and opened a hotel and restaurant here in town. It wasn't long before his hotel shut down due to the economy, but Francois was determined to keep his business afloat, so he started opening his kitchen to culinary students. Pretty soon he had so many interested pupils that he started using his hotel rooms for student housing, and the rest is history." He takes a deep breath and looks up. "Francois passed a lot of his success onto his students, and every president since has strived to continue that legacy. I hope y'all will take full advantage of everything our program has to offer. We have the finest instructors, and we are privileged to participate in various events and learning opportunities around the world." He grins and clears his throat. "Best of luck, everyone."

Mr. Dixon nods, and a few students start clapping as he slowly leaves the room. Professor Sellers helps him out the door before quickly taking his spot up front. He lifts his chin as he looks at us.

"Well, one of the first things Mr. Calle made was his famous peach pie," Professor Sellers continues.

"Famous?" a student comments. Professor Sellers nods and eyes the student in the back like he's about to pull out a detention slip. He seems to be the type of man who takes himself way more seriously than he should.

"Yes, you heard me correctly." He folds his arms and raises his eyebrows. "After the school became a success, Mr. Calle traveled back to France and prepared this exact dessert for the Queen's banquet."

Talk about intimidating.

"The queen?" I whisper. "Is he serious?"

Bree nods, but she doesn't whisper anything back.

"In a minute I will pass out a few recipe cards," Professor Sellers announces. "You'll have the rest of class today to make the school's traditional peach pie as best as you can. This will help me assess your current skill levels. And remember, mastering the goods we sell at the student bakery is essential to passing the program."

He begins passing out cards, starting with the front row. I take a good look at the ingredients and am surprised to see that almost all the ingredients are very basic. I scan the instructions and take a deep breath when I read how to make the pie dough. This will be my first attempt at making dough. *Cookie dough doesn't count.*

"What do you think?" I ask Bree. She looks over the recipe without any hint of fear in her eyes.

"Wow," she comments. "I would never have thought to use vanilla sugar." She promptly stands up and follows half the class to the storage room to gather ingredients. I read over the recipe a few times and close my eyes.

You can do this. It's only a pie. You can do this.

Professor Sellers returns from the pantry with his dry ingredients and immediately begins a demo on how to form pie dough. I watch as he mixes everything together so effortlessly and begins kneading the ball of dough in his bowl. He whips out his crust in minutes, and I have just barely found my measuring cups. I squint as I read them, making sure I'm using the right ones. I'd made the mistake once of using a tablespoon instead of a teaspoon or a teaspoon instead of a tablespoon. Those were a batch of oatmeal raisin cookies I will never forget.

"Here," Bree says. She lays ingredients in between us. "I got extra for you."

"Thanks." I grab a handful of fresh peaches that are said to have just arrived from a peach farm in Alabama.

"You might want to start your dough first," Bree mutters. "The dough needs time to rest."

"Of course," I reply. *Because like the rest of us, pie dough also needs a nap now and again.* I begin by cutting my butter into cubes.

"Smaller," Bree mutters.

"Like this?"

Bree nods but stops when she sees Professor Sellers glaring at us. I resume forming my dough on my own, hoping that I at least manage a tasty crust. I mix in the rest of my ingredients and begin working my dough. It's too sticky.

I add more flour and try again.

Now it's too stiff.

I do my best to form a ball with the dough before I put it aside.

"Don't worry too much about the lattice pattern on top," Professor Sellers comments. He is already rolling out his ball of dough and cutting it into long, thin strips.

"Lattice pattern?" I repeat. He raises an eyebrow as he looks at me. "*Of course*, the lattice pattern."

I immediately look down at my pie filling. I have no idea how big or how small to cut my peaches. I look over my shoulder and see Cole rolling his pie dough and measuring the thickness. I bite the inside of my cheek and do my best to finish.

This is going to take a lot more work than I thought.

* * *

The smell in the classroom is overwhelming. I am desperate to bite into a piece of Bree's pie because it looks absolutely perfect. She even managed to make the lattice pattern on top by weaving together strips of pie dough. She looked so comfortable when she did it. *Maybe she knits*? I wonder how many pies she has made. I am going to guess hundreds.

I look down at my pie and gulp when Professor Sellers pulls out a knife and a serving utensil. The sides of my pie are lumpy and some of the filling exploded out of the top while it was in the oven. It doesn't look as professional as all the others. I hope it at least tastes peachy.

"Okay," Professor Sellers says. "I am going to start with the front row. I will examine your pies, and as I do, I would like you to introduce yourself to the class." He walks over to a girl who arrived right after Bree and me and also took a spot up front. "Let's start with you, please."

"Hi, I'm Georgina." The woman has dirty blonde hair and a slender figure. She's wearing khaki pants and a light blue, button-down shirt under her apron. I look at her neck and wrist, surprised she's not also wearing pearls. "My family is from upstate New York, and they own a chain of specialty food stores. I plan on having my own brand of gourmet cake mixes. Well...*to start*."

She sports a fake smile as she looks around the room. Her smile turns a little sour when she spots me and looks down at the high-heeled boots I decided to wear to class, despite the fact that they stand out.

Professor Sellers studies a piece of her pie. He holds it up to check the thinness of her crust and thickness of her filling. He puts it down on a plate and takes a large bite. He nods before wiping his mouth.

"Nice filling to crust ratio," he comments. "Your pastry dough is light and fluffy. It could use a few more minutes in the oven, but other than that it's spot on, Georgina."

"Thank you, sir." Her eyes carefully examine Bree's pie like it is standing in her way of taking home a gold medal.

The professor moves onto Bree next. Bree clasps her hands below the counter and twiddles her thumbs. She is wearing tan colored dress pants and a floral blouse. Just like yesterday, I am the only one who decided to wear black this morning.

"Hi, I'm Bree. I'm from Connecticut, and I am the assistant head baker at a little cupcake shop by the coast. I made my first layered cake when I was five years old, and I have been hooked on sweets ever since." The professor looks at Bree and then studies her pie. He glances at Bree's face a second time as if he is memorizing our names according to his assessment of our pies. He definitely won't forget *my* name.

"Again, nice filling to crust ratio," Professor Sellers says. "And you did a great job with the lattice top. Bravo, Bree from Connecticut."

Bree's cheeks go rosy as she nods.

He looks at me next. His eyes go wide when they dart down to my pie. He looks up at me and briefly wrinkles his nose.

"Name?" he asks.

"Hi, I'm Poppy Peters. I'm from Portland, and I'm a former ballerina." I see Cole nod out of the corner of my eye. I gulp, feeling like I am center stage in a frivolous production of *Swan Lake*.

"Well, Poppy." Professor Sellers frowns when he looks at my pie. He slices a piece and holds it up so the whole class can see it. A bit of filling drips onto the counter. He reluctantly takes a small bite and looks at me. "Of course the filling isn't thick enough, and it's also too sweet. *Much* too sweet. The crust is too thick and way too dry. Traditionally one is sometimes offered a cup of coffee or a glass of milk with their pie. Not a whole gallon." I hear sniggers from classmates behind me.

"Oh," I sigh. "Okay." My shoulders slump on their own, but I immediately regain my straight posture.

"Better luck next time," Georgina comments. She looks at me sympathetically, but I know it's an act. As soon as Professor Sellers turns his head, her smile turns to a smirk. Her eyes dart from my pie to hers as she tucks a strand of hair behind her ear.

I am going to need some practice if I'm going to cut it here.

A lot of practice.

And maybe a pair of flats.

CHAPTER THREE

———

I'm a lightweight.

Bree introduced me to bourbon when we got back to our apartment. I needed to take my mind off my horrible first day of classes and having a second glass, *and third,* seemed like a good idea at the time. Not only did I fail at making the school's famous peach pie in Professor Sellers' class, but I also over-filled my pastry bag when Miss Chester asked us to practice our piping skills. Filling a doughnut shouldn't be that hard for a professional pastry student, but I splattered Bavarian cream all over her top.

"You're making it a bigger deal than it is," Bree says, sitting next to me at the kitchen table with her frozen, dinner-for-one meal of spicy chicken and rice. "No one even noticed what happened in Miss Chester's class."

I glare at her and gulp down the rest of my drink, hardly letting myself taste it. I cough and clear my throat before taking a few calming breaths. I already feel a bit queasy. Maybe that wasn't the *smartest* way to deal with my problems. I've made that mistake before. Once during my college years studying dance at Juilliard I overdid it when I found out that Jennifer Stevens had been given the lead role in the university's production of *Swan Lake*. I woke up the next morning near my gym locker with an empty box of my roommate's Fiendish Fancies that her mom had sent her from England, and a hangover from hell. I had rehearsed my butt off trying to snag that part.

"I seriously doubt that."

"Sit down and let me make you something with lots of chocolate." Bree raises her eyebrows as she looks at me. I realize that I am standing, and I feel a bit light-headed as my mind replays my disastrous first day over and over again.

"I should have sat in the back row," I mutter. "None of this would have happened if I'd sat in the back row."

"You just need a little practice, that's all." Bree takes another bite of her microwave dinner and chews it slowly. I take a step towards the front door, gazing out the window at the darkening sky. So far night is my favorite time of day. That's when it's cool enough to take a leisurely stroll without feeling like you're being baked in a giant oven.

"Practice," I repeat. "Yes, you're right. I need a do-over."

My feet take me to the front door. I step into the night air and breathe it in like my life depends on it. I can hear Bree yelling something from inside, but my brain can't translate it. I can only think of one thing. *My do-over.*

I walk along the sidewalk, passing all the apartments in our building. The moonlight illuminates my path. It shines through the billowing trees and makes them look like pieces of black licorice. I cross the quiet street and walk through campus. A soft breeze blows across my face, and my thoughts start to spin.

My first day was not how I expected it to be. I didn't think it would be easy, but I thought I would catch on eventually like Grandma Liz did. I remember her telling me how she was one of two women in her class. Watching her in the kitchen was like watching cupcakes rise in the oven. Every movement was natural, and every recipe came easily to her.

I run my fingers along a bench sitting beneath a tree and look at the building facing me. It's the building I spent all day in today. The one where I failed miserably at everything but introducing myself. Though I'm sure Professor Sellers had some sort of criticism about that too. He just didn't say it out loud.

I walk towards the building and quickly see that the door is propped open with a rock from the neighboring flowerbeds. My high-heeled boots echo slightly as I walk up a few steps and into the hallway where it all began. I feel the sudden urge to sit at my station and pretend that today went well. Maybe if I try really, really hard I can rewind time and try again.

I chuckle as I softly walk down the hallway and towards my classroom. The halls are dark except for moonlight that floods inside from between half-open blinds. I can't see where

I'm going very well, but I know my way. My class meets in the same student kitchens for the same classes every day of the week.

I take out my cell phone to light the rest of my way. The time says it's nearly midnight, but last time I looked at the time it was seven o'clock. That was before Bree pulled out her bottle of *false courage*. I drank too much of it. I shake my head and try to get rid of the image of my terrible peach pie. That dessert is going to haunt me until I get it right.

I reach our classroom, and my heart starts pounding.

I take a deep breath and pull at the door handle even though I know it won't open. I need a second chance at making that pie. Just one more chance. I know I can nail it like the rest of the class. I shake my head as I think about the way Professor Sellers looked at my pathetic pastry.

"It's too sweet." I mimic him out loud, curling my lips the way he did when he saw something distasteful. "Your crust is all *wrong*. Your filling is *wrong*. The way you combed your hair this morning is *wrong*. *Wrong*. *Wrong*. *Wrong* times a million."

I giggle to myself, but a sudden bang makes me jump. My heart starts racing, and my palms start sweating. I walk towards the noise with a lump in my throat. The noise is coming from one of the kitchens. When I hear another loud bang, I know I'm not crazy. It sounds like spoons hitting pots and pans. Maybe it's some sort of joke?

I take another step, but I stop myself from investigating any further. The school is dark, and the kitchens are locked. I don't know where the sound is coming from, but everyone has gone to bed. *Great, now I'm hearing things like my great grandpa Ed.*

BANG!

I hear the sound a third time, and my jaw clenches. My teeth grind together, and my hands squeeze themselves into tight fists. My calves are flexing, and my head starts spinning so fast that I think I might vomit. I see no light around me. No opens doors. No open windows.

"Hello?" I make a lame attempt at seeking a logical explanation for the noise. "Is someone there?"

Silence.

The hall is so quiet that I hear myself swallow.

I take a step backwards.

"Hello?" I say again.

I hear another noise, but this time it isn't banging, and it sounds closer. A gentle tap on the floor fills my ears, and I squint to make sure I'm seeing clearly. I see a shadow in front of me. It is close enough that my heart is racing out of control and far enough away that I can't tell if it's a person or a figment of my imagination.

I instinctively walk backwards until I'm far away from the mysterious blob at the end of the hall. I forget to breathe as I jog all the way back to my apartment and fumble with the key until I can open the front door. I let out a gasp and practically gulp down air.

It smells like Bree baked a batch of chocolate chip cookies after I left. I pop a chewy cookie into my mouth and resist the urge I have to wake Bree up and tell her what I saw. She might hate me if I do that. I rub my head, feeling a headache coming on. I need some sleep.

I go to my room and rest my head on my pillow. As soon as I close my eyes, the strange sound echoes through my memory. I cover my ears. I can't fall asleep. I sit up and contemplate eating another chocolate chip cookie. Bree might wake up to find that all her nervous baking sent me into a sugar coma.

I try to relax again.

I have to force myself to rest up for tomorrow. The same way that snooty girl, Georgina, forced herself to smile at me when Professor Sellers was watching. *That's it*. I have to pretend that today didn't faze me at all and that I *do* have what it takes to cut it at Calle Pastry Academy. I have to focus on being fake tomorrow just like Georgina.

* * *

A hand shakes my shoulder. I gasp as I wake up. My heart pounds when I open my eyes. I see Bree jump back looking startled. She gulps as she hands me a mug of coffee. I take a swig of it before I do anything else. I cringe.

"Ahhh," I blurt out. "Why is it cold?"

"It was hot the first time I tried to wake you up," she comments, shaking her head. She places a hand on her hip and eyes a pair of jeans I left on the floor.

"Why do I feel like I've moved back in with my parents?" I mutter quietly.

"Come on." Bree hands me an aspirin. "We can't be late for our orientation of the student bakery at 6 a.m. It's a very important part of the program, remember?"

"That's today?" I almost trip as I race to my suitcase and pull out a pair of shorts.

"I'll wait for five more minutes, but then I have to get going," she responds.

I quickly get dressed and meet Bree outside. We begin the quick walk to the student bakery on the other side of campus. By the time we arrive the sun is peeking over the clouds, and I'm sweaty enough to say I've been for a morning jog.

We join a group of students, and I catch my breath. I haven't gotten up this early since I was cast as Clara in *The Nutcracker Ballet*. I remember secretly wanting to eat the costume that was made for the scene with Mother Ginger. It was made of real gingerbread and vanilla icing. I didn't care that it was rock hard.

"You survived," a voice says behind me. I turn and see Cole. He is wide awake.

"Gosh, what's your secret?" I ask.

"To looking good?" He straightens the collar on his shirt. It is baby blue with tiny, white stripes. His sleeves are rolled up and he's wearing light khaki slacks. "It comes naturally."

"For getting up this early," I correct him. I glance at the other students in my class and see that they are all dressed like they are giving business presentations.

"This is nothing," he replies. "The students who are running the bakery have to show up at 3."

My eyes go wide.

"As in *3 a.m.*?"

"Uh-huh. That will be us next semester."

I twiddle my fingers as I look down at my casual choice of shorts and a T-shirt. I assumed that my apron would cover everything anyway, but I still feel silly. I rub my forehead, hoping that the aspirin I took will kick in soon.

An old man walks slowly to meet us in front of the student bakery with a cup of coffee in his hand. The man is short and plump with silvery hair. He walks with a slight limp as he meets our group with a tired stare on his face. He nods and takes a sip of his coffee.

"Where can *we* get a shot of caffeine?" I mutter.

"How much coffee do you actually drink in one day?" Cole asks. He chuckles when I shrug.

Always having coffee on hand, whether or not I drink it, is habit. I blame it on years of late night rehearsals and random spurts of insomnia brought about by overtraining.

"Shush," I reply. "Mr. Teacher is speaking."

"Morning," the man says in a scratchy voice. He clears his throat. "I am your kitchen management teacher, Professor Harris. Just call me Mr. Harris. I've been here at this school as long as I can remember." He pauses to scratch a spot on his head where his hair is thinning. "Well, let's get on with it." He opens the doors to the bakery. It doesn't open for a couple of hours, but I can hear commotion in the kitchen. The first thing that hits me when I walk through the doors is the smell of pie. It makes my stomach rumble, but it also reminds me of yesterday.

Forget yesterday and move on, Poppy.

The front of the bakery is still dark, and the café chairs are still turned upside down on the tables. I watch Bree move towards the front of our group. I linger near the back with Cole. Today I'm lying low.

"He's quite the cheerful one," I quietly comment.

"Oh, yeah," Cole murmurs.

He folds his arms and takes a deep breath as we follow our classmates into the kitchen. It's bigger than the kitchen in our classroom on campus. Underneath and above the counters are stacks of pans in every shape and size. I wipe a bead of sweat from my brow. With all the ovens on I feel like I'm still outside. A student in a white bakery uniform brushes past me to grab a mixer on the shelf behind me.

"Does anyone else feel like they're in the way?" I comment.

A few students look back at me, annoyed.

I decide to keep my mouth shut for a while.

"Dang, Lil' Mama," Cole whispers. "Looks like you've already made a few enemies."

Starting with her Highness of NYC, the all-around perfect Georgina.

Another student working at the bakery brushes past us for another bundle of tools. Cole and I take a few steps back until we're leaning up against a counter. Someone bumps the side of my leg. I reach down and rub the spot that might potentially be bruised in the morning.

"Sorry," someone whispers. I look up and see a man with blond hair and ice blue eyes towering over me. "I didn't mean to bump you." He folds his arms and reveals a set of bulky biceps. The fabric of his sleeve slightly touches me, and it sends my heart racing.

"Oh, it's okay," I lie. I smile and feel myself blushing. Luckily, I can blame it on the heat in the kitchen.

"I'm Jeff," he says quietly.

"Poppy."

"Yes, I know." He grins. "I remember from yesterday."

"Right," I respond. "My epic pie failure."

"Come on, it wasn't *that* bad. I once a dated a girl who thought potatoes were called *fry balls.* At least you know the basics." He pauses. "And that fries are made from potatoes."

I laugh.

"You *do* know that, right?" he jokes.

"I do now," I reply. His eyes linger on the curves of my face as he grins.

Mr. Harris clears his throat as he puts his hand on the shoulder of a tall student in a white uniform. The student is covered in flour. He also has a half smile, and his eyes are darting from us to the bread ovens. He opens his mouth when a timer starts chirping, but he quickly closes it as another student rushes to take care of it.

"This is Steve, the head baker this semester."

"Only because Tom's gone," Steve chuckles, folding his arms. The smirk disappears from his face when he notices the stern way that Mr. Harris is looking at him.

"Uh, excuse me," I call out. "Do you mean Tom as in Tom Fox?"

"Yes," Steve answers. Mr. Harris narrows his eyes and looks at me, singling me out. He tightens his hold on Steve's shoulder and glares at him like he's seconds away from being handed a detention slip. "Sorry, sir."

"Everyone, Steve," he repeats. "Steve, this is everyone. Go ahead." Mr. Harris looks to Steve to finish the rest of his introduction. As soon as Steve catches on, Mr. Harris takes a few steps back to finish his morning coffee. I watch him discreetly snag a scone and nibble on the end as Steve starts pointing out things in the kitchen.

"Okay," Steve says. "Well, the ovens are over there, and we all rotate stations. So basically you will all get the chance to make everything we sell. You'll also take a turn washing dishes."

A few students groan.

"Hey," Steve continues. "You can't mess that up, so it's not so bad."

I see Georgina glance back at me.

"Some of us might," Georgina mutters.

I contemplate sticking out my tongue at her like a five-year-old, but I decide against it. Besides, Jeff is standing right next to me.

The sound of pots and pans banging grabs my attention. I look over and see a couple of students working on beignet batter. My mind jumps back to last night. My chest starts pounding and not because Jeff looked at me again.

"Beignets are made over here," Steve says, leading us through the bustling kitchen. "We use certain bowls to make our special blend of homemade brown sugar and spices." He holds up a mixing bowl with an emblem of the school on it. "The founder of CPA had these made for his trip to France."

"What do you make over there?" a student asks, just as a bowl of batter accidentally drops to the floor.

"Really, Bramley?" Steve whines. "That's the second time this morning." He rushes to help the student clean up the mess before anyone steps in it. I feel stupid watching and not helping, but I can hardly move where I am standing.

"Shouldn't we help them?" I mutter.

"You'll get your turn to clean up messes, don't worry," Georgina states. A couple of girls next to her giggle.

"This is where we make our signature Buzz's Rise and Shine Orange Rolls," Steve says, wiping the last of the spilled batter. I smile as I think of how good that orange roll tasted when I tried it.

"Who is Buzz?" a student asks.

Steve smiles.

"I am glad you asked," he replies "Buzz was the nickname for the founder's son. The kitchen hands used to call him Buzz, but his real name was Thomas or *Old Man Thomas*. He came up with this recipe for orange rolls as a cover up when he accidentally ordered a double delivery of oranges. He didn't want to tell his dad he had made a mistake, so he made these rolls as if he ordered the oranges on purpose."

"Nice save," Cole chuckles.

The same student raises her hand.

"What happened to Buzz? Is his family still around?" the student asks.

"He's dead," Steve says bluntly. "He went missing one night, and no one knows what happened to him."

Everyone glances at each other with confused looks on their faces.

"I guess we will never know," I say out loud.

"Oh," Steve adds. "I can't believe I almost forgot this, but Old Man Thomas's ghost haunts the school. Or so people say. The legend is that you can hear him banging around in the kitchens late at night, but no one has seen his ghost in years."

"Or maybe no one is stupid enough to tell people they're seeing things that aren't there," Georgina says boldly. She laughs and lifts her chin. Her blonde ponytail bounces around as she does.

I swallow the lump in my throat. The group continues walking through the kitchen, but I stay frozen in place. Cole stays behind and nudges me. I look at him and keep walking.

"What's wrong?" he whispers.

"I think I heard a ghost last night," I admit.

"You should have come out with me and my roommate." Cole slowly follows our group to one of the store rooms. I'm almost elbowed in the gut by a student whipping meringue.

"I'm not joking," I mutter. "I saw something last night near our classroom."

"What were you doing over there?" he asks.

I hear another bang that makes my head throb. I think about last night and how the shadowy figure stared at me from the end of the hallway while I stood frozen and a little drunk. I look over my shoulder and see someone using one of the school's specially-made bowls to mix sugar with molasses. The student pauses to add a few spices and then continues mixing vigorously.

"Never mind that." I clear my throat. "There was someone in the kitchens last night."

"Did you see who it was?" Cole narrows his eyes as he looks at me.

"I couldn't see a face but—"

"You didn't see Old Man Thomas, Poppy." He chuckles and shakes his head. "I'm sure it was just someone trying get ahead on cake construction or something."

"No," I whisper. "Whoever it was just *appeared* out of nowhere."

"No one appears out of nowhere," he argues. "I'm sure there's a logical explanation."

"You're right," I say sarcastically. "It must have been Georgina mixing up gourmet cake recipes for her debut baking line."

Georgina's head tilts when I say her name. She swiftly glances over her shoulder and glares at me before directing her attention back to Steve. I cover my mouth with my hand as Steve, the head baker, points to the various pantry items that are stored in airtight containers.

"What was that about?" Cole whispers. I wait until Georgina's attention is focused solely on Steve's presentation.

"Her ears must have been burning."

For the rest of our tour we observe the many stations where each pastry is made. My mouth waters when a hot pan of orange rolls is pulled from the oven and frosted with orange glaze. The sweet frosting melts perfectly over each bun. Mr.

Harris snags one and takes a bite like it's a completely normal thing to do. He does the same with the other pastries, and just when I think he can't bear to stomach any more he nibbles at the first piece of peach pie. In truth, Mr. Harris did the things we all wished we could do if it weren't socially inappropriate. But then we would all be his size. Plump and round like a ripe nectarine.

"Mr. Harris, will we be tested on all this?" Georgina raises her hand but speaks freely when Mr. Harris looks at her. He looks bothered that she's even asking that question.

"Does it matter?" he responds.

"It matters to me." She raises her eyebrows as if his retort is inappropriate.

"Not everything is a test, silly girl," he murmurs. He coughs to clear his scratchy voice.

"Excuse me?" Georgina bites back. She places her hands on her hips. "Mr. Harris, I'm paying good money to attend this program. My family has built a successful business in the food industry from nothing, and our company was even listed as one of Oprah's Favorite Things. That's right. *Oprah.* What qualifies you to sit there choking down pie and refer to me as a silly, little girl?"

The entire class and most of the kitchen goes silent as Mr. Harris clenches his jaw. He springs forward so quickly that it startles me. His round body moves from its spot near the hot pastry counter in a flash. Georgina takes a step back trying to play it cool, but she's blushing.

"What qualifies me?" he shouts. "What qualifies *me?*" Beads of sweat form on his forehead, and his entire face looks as if it might light on fire. "I've prepared meals for hundreds of thousands of soldiers back when I served in the army. *I* have earned the right to teach as I please."

Georgina nods. She firmly clasps her hands together.

"My apologies," she gulps.

Mr. Harris growls and storms out of the kitchen. I've met men like him before. Men with a short fuse. I suppose seeing certain things from the front lines, or from the cook's line, can scar a person for life. My dad once did business with a captain in the Navy who dove to the floor during lunch after a plate shattered in the kitchen. He thought he was being shot at.

"Remind me never to piss him off," Cole says quietly.

I wipe another bead of sweat from my forehead after Jeff nods in my direction. I follow Cole back outside just as the sun is starting to rise. It turns the sky an orangey color that reminds me again of orange-scented sticky buns. I clutch my stomach to stop it from making loud noises. At least one good thing came of this bakery orientation. I met Jeff.

"Ready?" Bree finally joins me again as our class breaks up across the quad before our morning lessons.

"Ready for what?"

"Day two," she responds. "We still have a full day of classes ahead of us."

"But our first one isn't until ten this morning, right?"

I feel relieved when Bree nods. That means I can head back to our apartment and sleep off my headache. The two of us walk back to our apartment. Bree makes another pot of coffee, and I collapse on my bed and close my eyes. Day two *cannot* be like day one. I have to try harder.

I have to wear flats.

CHAPTER FOUR

———

My eyes open to the sound of chirping. I sit up quickly and glance around my room. I didn't bring an alarm clock. I check my phone. It's almost time for class. I stand up and move towards my dresser, and the chirping stops. I scratch my head and take a few steps back again.

Chirp. Chirp. Chirp.

It sounds like a cricket, but sunlight is streaming through my window. I rub my eyes and rummage through my suitcase for something more presentable to wear to class. Something that helps me fit in instead of stand out. I own way too many yoga pants, and I know that Georgina would find a way to poke fun at me if I wore a skirt and high heels.

I settle on my only pair of khakis and a silky, emerald green top. It kills me to slip into my only pair of ballet flats, but I force myself to do it when I hear Bree grabbing her bag in the living room. I jog to meet her before she leaves without me.

"Do I look the part?" I ask.

Bree looks me up and down with a wide smile. Her wavy, strawberry blonde hair is tied up in a bun, and she's wearing the same peach colored button-down that she wore this morning for our bakery tour.

"Well, you're not wearing black for once," she replies. "But I never thought there was anything wrong with the way you dress."

"I'm going for a fresh start."

"On day two?" She raises her eyebrows.

"Okay," I sigh. "Just promise me something..."

"Anything." Bree shuts and locks our front door. We begin our walk across campus to the student kitchens.

"If today goes like yesterday did, keep your bourbon to yourself." I straighten my top as we walk. My heart is racing and my stomach churning as I think about the look on Professor Sellers face when he sees that I've come back for more.

"Honey, I warned you that a little taste would be plenty for you." She reaches into her bag and pulls out a double chocolate chip cookie wrapped in plastic wrap. She hands one to me. "Chocolate?"

I smile.

"I think we were destined to be roommates." I take the cookie and unwrap it. "Also, I think there's a cricket trapped behind my dresser. It seems to have gotten confused between night and day. It wouldn't stop chirping this morning."

Bree laughs as we stroll towards our building. I glance at the front entrance, and it brings back flashes of hazy memories. I remember the door being propped open last night. My eyes dart to a bed of flowers next to the front windows. I spot a few rocks among the dirt.

"Poppy?" Bree says, gazing at me suspiciously.

I am standing in the doorway with my fists clenched together.

"Sorry." I shake my head. "Got lost in thought for a minute there."

"Uh-huh." Bree's eyes stay wide as she turns and casually walks into our classroom.

When my eyes wander down the hallway, a burst of adrenaline soars through my chest. My heart starts pounding, and my palms feel sweaty. Part of me is expecting to see something lurking in the farthest corner looking back at me. I lift my chin and think of Grandma Liz. *What would Grandma Liz do?*

For starters, Grandma wouldn't let a bossy little tart like Georgina make her feel like she didn't belong. I've worked just as hard as these people. It might not have been in the same subjects, but I've still come a long way to be here. Literally.

Bree and I are not the first students to arrive. Most of my classmates are sitting at the same stations as yesterday. I reluctantly take my spot up front next to Bree and pull open my tote bag. I pull out a pen and my notebook and review my notes from yesterday.

Don't over-sweeten.
Don't over-salt.
Don't call Professor Sellers Mr. Sellers or Stuart.

I read the same notes over and over again until I hear the sound of Professor Sellers zipping up his chef's jacket. He walks to his table at the front of the class with a tray of cupcakes. In most situations, a tray of cupcakes is a good thing – a symbol of celebration or a treat on a special occasion. I remember licking the frosting off of the tres leches cupcakes Grandma Liz made for my sixth birthday party. I almost got away with it too.

Professor Sellers is the only man I've met that can make a sweet thing like a petite, vanilla cupcake look like a punishment.

He sets the tray down and arranges the cakes in a straight line so we can see them all. He pulls out a knife and sets it down on the table. I gulp when he looks around the room, afraid that he might scowl when he sees my face. I didn't exactly make a good first impression with any of my teachers.

"Today we are going to start with the basics," he announces. His eyes briefly look in my direction. "The *very* basics." He pauses and clears his throat. "Here we have a dozen cupcakes, but they aren't just ordinary cupcakes. I've prepared the cakes and frostings using different consistencies to show you how to manipulate your batter."

He stops and chooses a cupcake. He gently takes his knife and slices it in half, showing us the inside. The frosting looks a little flat compared to the others, and the cake is smaller. I take a deep breath. I can do this. I can bake cupcakes from scratch. I've done it before, and I can do it again. Why didn't we start with this yesterday?

"This is not an ideal cake," he continues. "Who can tell me why just by looking at it?"

Bree is the first one to raise her hand.

"The frosting looks too thin," she answers. "And the cake looks really dense. Almost like a bread. Most people assume that dense cake is caused by using too much flour, but it actually happens when you use too much of your wet ingredients. We definitely wouldn't sell that in the cupcake shop where I worked back home."

"Exactly right," Professor Sellers agrees.

"And it looks like the cake was still warm when it was frosted," Bree adds. "I've made that mistake myself before."

"You are correct." The professor moves on to another cake. He cuts it in half and holds it up for everyone to observe. "As you can see, the texture of this cake is more like a sponge. The frosting however is too stiff." He moves a piece of frosting with his finger. "See how it creates more and more crumbs when I try to smooth it down? The frosting needs more liquid."

He sets the cupcake down and holds up another one.

"See this one." He peels back the wrapper. "This one has the perfect ratio of frosting to cake. The frosting isn't too sweet, and it's a medium consistency. The cake is also light and airy." He takes a bite of the vanilla cupcake and smirks. "Perfect." He licks his lips and swallows before speaking again. "By the end of the day I expect a dozen cupcakes that look just like this. Turn to page ten in your booklets. You may use any cake recipe you like. Remember that cocoa powder can dry out a cake faster."

"I'll make chocolate and you make vanilla," Bree mutters. "That way we have two flavors when we take the leftovers home."

"Vanilla." I nod. "Okay, I can do vanilla."

"For those of you who did the assigned reading, this shouldn't be too hard." Professor Sellers gives us the okay to start baking. "We will discuss our batters in more detail later. You have one hour to get your batters ready for the ovens. That should be plenty of time." He glances at me as he walks around the classroom.

I open my recipe booklet containing a bunch of basic recipes that we will be using over the course of the program. We all received them yesterday, and I was overwhelmed when I flipped through mine and saw things like crème filled éclairs with a salted caramel drizzle and pistachio encrusted cherry cheesecake.

"Vanilla, huh?" a voice says over my shoulder. I turn and see Jeff grinning behind me. His blond hair is combed back, and his icy blue eyes gleam more than ever in the morning sunlight that is coming in through the blinds.

"Yeah," I reply. "Thought I'd stick to the basics. You know."

Georgina brushes past me and glances at Jeff as he leans on the counter. Her gaze turns sour when it moves to me. She brushes her hair over shoulder and keeps walking.

"I'm sure you'll be fine," Jeff responds, barely noticing Georgina's little once-over. "They're only cupcakes. I'm sure you could do this in your sleep, am I right?"

Jeff's attempt to make me feel better is only making it worse. I have baked cupcakes before but not as often as he has, I'm sure. Cupcakes weren't really something on the menu for me until I left the world of ballet. I bite the corner of my lip.

"I've got this," I say. Whether or not it's true, I choose to believe that it is.

I read over the list of ingredients that I'll need for vanilla cupcakes and gather the things I'll need from the pantry. Bree is already preparing her bowl of dry ingredients. She gently spoons in her cocoa powder, careful not to use too much.

"Hey, Jeff," Georgina says from across the room. Her expression is perkier than usual, and she's sticking her chest out as she waits for him to look up and notice her. "You're a tall guy. Will you grab that mixer for me on the top shelf?"

"Sure." Jeff lightly taps my counter before he walks away to help Georgina.

"Is it just me, or does everyone on our group seem to be single?" Bree whispers. I had no idea that she had been watching Jeff and me the whole time.

"Well, *someone* is definitely on the prowl," I mutter, glancing up as Georgina touches Jeff's arm while she says thank you. "My parents would be ecstatic if I told them I've met someone here. All my mom talks about these days is how she'll never be a grandma."

"My mom is the opposite," Bree says quietly. "She says all men are scum. Of course, she is always referring to my *father* when she says it."

"Since when did it become a crime to enter your thirties without a husband or boyfriend?"

"I guess that makes me a criminal." Bree shrugs.

I concentrate on my batter. I mix my dry ingredients and my wet ingredients in separate bowls before blending them together. I read through my recipe again to make sure I have everything right. I watch Bree scoop her batter into muffin tins. Each tin has the same amount of chocolate batter. I copy her exact movements until I'm looking at the perfect specimen. I show my cupcakes to Bree, and she nods approvingly.

"All you have to do now is make sure they aren't undercooked," Bree comments. "Or overcooked."

"You really think they look good?"

"See." Bree follows me to an open oven. "Yesterday was a total fluke."

I preheat my oven, and Bree finds another one because her chocolate cakes bake at a different temperature. I wait until my oven beeps before sliding my cupcake pan onto the baking rack. I shut the oven door and carefully set my timer.

Georgina snags an oven next to mine. She glances down into my oven and raises her eyebrows. I open my mouth to say something to her – something that might get me kicked out of class, but I decide not to. Over the years, I've learned the hard way that it's better to hold your tongue than lay it all out on the table. Maybe the more I observe Georgina and what makes her tick, the less upset she will make me.

Nah.

Something that makes Georgina tick at the moment is Jeff. Georgina spends a little too much time bending over as she places her pan of batter into her oven. When she stands up straight again she discreetly looks over her shoulder to where Jeff is sitting. He didn't take the bait.

I cover my mouth and hold in a giggle, but it comes out anyway. Georgina's head jerks in my direction and for a split second, her cheeks turn rosy. She glares at me the way she has since the first moment she laid eyes on me.

"Is something funny?" she asks. Her long, blonde ponytail bounces from side to side when she tilts her head.

"Oh, it's nothing."

"A little advice," she continues. Her eyes dart to my oven. "Spend less time flirting and more time studying, and maybe you'll actually have a shot at passing this course."

"Good advice," I reply, walking past her to wait at my station. "But lucky for me, I'm really, *really* good at multi-tasking."

I hurry back to my station before Georgina has the chance to come up with another snotty remark about my famous pie failure yesterday. Bree washes her hands and sits next to me. I open my notebook and begin doodling a picture of a blooming flower.

"Uh, why does Georgina look like she just walked past an outhouse?" Bree whispers.

"I'll tell you later."

I read through my textbook and get caught up on the chemistry behind yeast. Bree reads alongside me, eagerly waiting for her oven timer to go off. As timers chirp, Bree or Georgina jump up and yell the oven number. When Bree's chocolate cupcakes are done I hear her giggle with delight as she pulls them out to cool. I put my head down and read a few more pages before another sound fills the classroom.

But it's not chirping.

"Oh, great!" Professor Sellers runs to the oven where the fire alarm is going off. I see smoke emerging from an oven, and the professor is shouting for someone to grab a fire extinguisher. Jeff and Cole leap out their chairs and run to fetch it.

"We've got to kill this smoke before—" The professor's sentence is cut off by the sound of Georgina squealing. The smoke persists long enough to set off the safety sprinklers. Water pours from the ceiling, forcing everyone to flee from the classroom.

"Ugh! My hair!" Georgina is the first person to roll her eyes and leave. I grab my bag and follow Bree outside. The rest of the classrooms empty, and the quad fills up with bewildered students. I squeeze the water from my long, damp hair and hope that my makeup isn't so smudged that I have raccoon eyes.

Professor Sellers emerges from the building with the other professors. He mutters a few things to them and then nods. He faces our class and folds his arms, disappointed. A siren blasts from down the street, and another professor runs to meet it.

"Okay," Professor Sellers says so that everyone can hear him. "Who had oven number three? The temperature was turned on much too high, and the oven timer wasn't even on."

My throat tightens, and I feel as if I might choke. My toes curl up inside my shoes as I hang my head and take a deep breath. *I* had oven number three, but I set it to the correct temperature, and I distinctly remember setting my timer. With damp hair and wet clothes, I step forward and discreetly hold up my hand.

"Ah, yes," he responds. "Come with me, Ms. Peters."

The quad falls silent as I follow him past a parked fire engine and around the corner where none of the other students can see us. I brace myself for what might happen next. At least he doesn't have the authority to expel me.

At least, I don't think he does.

"Ms. Peters," he says quietly.

"Poppy," I correct him.

"Poppy." He clasps his hands together. "Why on earth did you set your oven so high?"

"But I didn't—"

"If you can't even set an oven, I'm astounded that you got into this school at all," he continues.

"But, Professor—"

"Let me finish," he snaps. "You are on very thin ice right now. I am going to be paying close attention to you from now on just to make sure nothing like this happens again, and I suggest you spend *every* night practicing the basics in your apartment, understand?"

"Yes," I answer.

"Good." He leaves me and heads towards the fire engine parked alongside the building.

Professor Sellers just gave me a second chance, but I feel as defeated as ever. I had everything down this time. Everything. My batter was perfect. The way I filled my cupcake pan was perfect. My oven settings were perfect. In fact, I followed every rule to the letter so that the only way this could have happened was if someone changed something.

She wouldn't, would she?

I think of the one person who has a reason to hate me right now. The same person who had a moment alone with my cupcakes. *Georgina.*

I'm not sure why Georgina would stoop so low that she would risk sending the entire building up in flames. I would never do a thing like that. I walk slowly back towards the crowd of people outside the building, and when I do most of them quiet down. I hate that feeling you get when you know someone is whispering about you. I concentrate on my steps, trying hard not to blush. I avoid eye contact with Georgina.

"So," Bree gulps. "What did he say?"

"He gave me a warning."

"Thank heavens," she mutters.

"But that isn't the worst of our problems." I glance around and see Cole staring in my direction. I smile at him, letting him know that things are okay.

"You did everything right." Bree shakes her head looking confused. "I know you did. I saw you."

"*Someone* turned up the heat," I respond.

"Who?" she gasps.

"Who do you think?"

"Why that crazy little—"

"Not here," I cut Bree off before she starts cussing Georgina out in front of everyone. Though Bree shouting profanities in one of her sundresses is something I hope to see one day.

"Poppy, you've got to get her back."

"I will," I reassure her. "I will in time."

CHAPTER FIVE

I pace our living room thinking of what to do next. All the times in my life that I've confronted people it never went down so well. The last time I did that was with my ex-boyfriend. My chest is pounding, and I can't stop thinking about what happened today. My cupcake failure will be the talk of the school for years and years to come.

"I'm relieved that you weren't expelled," Bree sighs. She is flipping through a magazine looking for a good recipe for dinner. Comfort food. "I insist that we eat our feelings tonight."

"Well, if you insist," I respond.

"Macaroni and cheese?" she suggests.

"Maybe we should go out?"

"First you need to figure out what to do about Georgina," Bree comments. She sets her magazine down on the coffee table and frowns. "I say you turn her in. That little brat could use a good slap on the wrist."

"No." I laugh. "A talking to won't shake up a girl like Georgina."

"It sure as heck would scare the crap out of me. I'm just saying." Bree stands up and heads for the kitchen.

"No we need something…" I think back to the few times in my life when I've actually plotted and sought revenge against someone else. Those plans always backfired "No." I sigh.

"Turn her in," Bree says again. "That's what I would do."

"The one thing that would piss Georgina off the most would be if I actually graduated with her."

"What are you saying? You're going to let her get away with it?"

"I'm saying I'm going to study extra hard until I get this right," I answer. "I'm going to keep my head down and do my work. That's how I'm going to get back at her."

Bree looks at me and rolls her eyes. She opens a cupboard and pulls out a container of flour. She's at it again. The nervous baking. But for how often she whips together a layered cake or a batch of chocolate chip cookies, she must be a nervous wreck twenty-four/seven.

I guess everyone has issues. Even perfectionists like Bree.

* * *

Weeks go by and I avoid the school kitchens like a batch of burnt brownies. The only time I'm there is during the day when everyone else is practicing their piping techniques. I'm not allowed to practice anything involving the ovens after hours without a buddy. *Kind of humiliating.* I've been studying with Bree, but the pressure to be perfect and not screw up again eats away at me. So far I'm not doing so hot, though Bree disagrees. She says I'm doing just fine for a beginner. I never thought that frosting a layered cake or piping macaron batter into a perfect circle would be so difficult.

How did Grandma Liz do it all?

I scratch the side of my head and check my dough again for my cinnamon rolls. They are part of a simple lesson to teach us the proper way to use yeast. My dough still won't rise. I slump my shoulders and shake my head. I feel a hand on my arm. I turn and see Jeff studying my dough. He kneads it a little and then looks at me.

"Your water must have been too hot," he comments.

"Story of my life," I sigh.

"Don't bother, Jeff," I hear Georgina say. She walks past with a perfectly positioned pan of fluffy cinnamon rolls. "This one is slowly realizing that dancers don't belong in the kitchen."

"Oh, you—"

"Poppy," Bree cuts in. Her cheeks are red, and she jerks me away from Georgina's pan. "Don't, honey."

"What?" I say. "It's not like I'm going to knock the pan right out of her hands."

That is exactly what I want to do. After the sprinkler fiasco, I did exactly what I said I was going to do. I ignored Georgina and focused on my studies. For a few days, Georgina avoided me too. I was starting to think that something inside her actually felt guilty for setting me up like that.

That all changed a couple days ago when Jeff started dragging his stool over to my station to share my book.

"Ignore her," Bree instructs me. She has been the ice water that drenches my fire since day one. Bree and Cole are the people I feel most comfortable with. They get me.

"Do you know what you need?" Jeff says. I shift from side to side in my heels. Professor Sellers told me that wearing heels to class all the time wasn't the practical thing to do, but I miss them when they aren't on my feet. I noticed right away that I wasn't the only shoe addict on campus. Most girls bring another set of shoes in their tote bags. I forgot mine today, so I'm stuck wearing heels for the rest of the lesson.

"A handheld fan?" I guess, wiping my forehead.

"Some time off," he says.

My stomach churns as he grins and stares at the splotches of icing on my apron. I know where this is going, and I was hoping I would have more time.

"Oh."

"Let me take you out," he continues. *Georgina is going to flip a lid.* My heart leaps, but being asked out only reminds me of the doughnut hole of an ex-boyfriend I left behind in Oregon. While I traveled across the country going on auditions, he was making his rounds, too, at Bailey Gentlemen's Club. A girl with really pink lipstick named Candi was kind enough to fill me in one Sunday morning.

"Tonight?"

"Yes, tonight." Jeff chuckles. "I will pick you up at seven, okay?"

"Perfect," I lie. He has been nice to me since day one, and I am attracted to him. I don't have the guts to tell him, *No, I would rather stay home and read* Southern Living *with my roomie.*

As soon as he walks away, Bree nudges me. Her face is glowing. I frown as I watch her clean up her station. I should have mastered the basics by now, but I am still struggling, and I can't figure out why. I sat down and thought about it a million times. In Oregon, I baked cakes and rolled dough without any problems. This is what I've *always* wanted to do, and after my first two days here I promised myself that I would *never* let anything like that happen again. No more epic failures.

I don't understand what is holding me back.

"Oh, my gosh," Bree says under her breath. "I thought he would never ask."

"Huh?"

Half the class leaves after finishing their assignment. As usual I am one of the last students left. Bree takes her time cleaning up her station and then starts reading one of her textbooks as I cut my rolls. I shape them on the pan and let them rise a little longer.

As much as they *can* rise since I seemed to have killed my yeast.

"You know, I stand by what I said our first day," Cole says, walking up behind me. He glances at my baking project. "If you need help, I'll tutor you."

"I keep offering, but she's stubborn," Bree comments.

"I know," Cole says. "I don't get it. She's so close to academic probation, and yet she lives with the buttercream queen."

Bree smiles at the compliment and slowly shakes her head like I'm hopeless.

"Hi," I cut in. "I'm right here, and I am trying my best to get through this semester on my own."

"You've got to stop freezing up when you're asked to do demonstrations," Cole says.

"I did nearly set the building on fire my second day here, remember?"

"That wasn't your fault," Bree says.

"No, but...*day one*. Remember *day one*? My horrific peach pie?"

"Is she serious?" Cole says, looking at Bree. "Poppy, you need to let that go. For as long as you let that memory haunt you, it will."

I take a deep breath and face the inevitable. Cole is right. I do need help if I'm going to pass all my basic level courses. I frown. Grandma never mentioned that this program was so hard. Maybe I just don't have the talent for it that she did?

"Fine," I agree. "I'll meet you here tonight after dinner."

Cole grins and straightens the collar of his light orange button-down. The color reminds me of an orange Creamsicle.

One of those sounds really good right now.

"Don't keep her too long, Cole." Bree smirks as she gathers her books and places them in her bag. "She's got a *date*."

"With who?" Cole looks a little disappointed. "There's no time for dating at CPA. Are you crazy?"

"Chill," I respond. "It's just dinner. I think."

"That's how it starts anyway," Bree quietly comments. I stare at her for a moment, but decide against asking her to elaborate. We have all had boyfriend issues at one point or another. I don't care to bring mine up. Ever.

"I'll keep that in mind," I say. I turn back to Cole. "Give me an hour."

"You got it."

* * *

Cole is a genius.

We practice for one of our upcoming tests by re-creating a few pastries that the student bakery sells. I fill my éclairs, pleased with myself for finally getting the dough right. Cole watches me to make sure I don't overfill them.

It is getting late, and the two of us are alone in the student kitchens. I am so proud of myself for making the perfect éclairs that I forget all about the past couple of weeks, and how I was almost expelled for something I didn't do.

"You know," I comment. "I think I can tackle that peach pie again. I don't know what was going through my head that day."

"I do," Cole replies. He changes his expression and attempts to mimic me using a high-pitched voice. "Is there AC in here? There better be AC in here or I'll—"

I hit his arm.

"What?" I take a bite of my finished éclair and lick the chocolate from my lips. There's nothing better than being able to taste your success. "It's hot here. Maybe I'm cold-blooded and just never noticed it before?"

"My aunt makes these sometimes in casserole form," he says, taking another bite of his éclair.

"You're kidding."

"Nope." He takes another huge bite and nods. "She calls it éclair pie. It's basically graham crackers, French vanilla pudding, and chocolate sauce layered in a casserole dish."

"Your aunt sounds amazing."

"She doesn't live far from here," he says. "I think I'll be going to see her during our holiday break."

"Nice. I'll be flying back West and, unfortunately, staying with my parents. My apartment there is being rented at the moment." I sigh and gaze around at the empty classroom. The storage room is dark like the halls outside. The only light around us is coming from the fixture right above our heads. "Should be interesting."

"Three days is my max when I go see my mom. Once that line is crossed she goes back to hollering at me for leaving my socks on the floor."

"I'm sure you're incredibly messy, Cole. I don't blame her."

"Oh, I see," he jokes. "Take her side."

I laugh and lick a bit of chocolate from my pastry. Why can't every class feel like this? Calm. Comfortable. Easy. Or maybe it's having Cole around that helps me relax?

"Well, at least all that time back in my old room will give me some time to do some serious thinking," I say quietly.

"Quit second guessing yourself." Cole notices my frustration and shakes his head. "You deserve to be here just as much as anyone else."

"If only I was good enough to come up with my own line of gourmet cake mixes," I joke.

Cole chuckles and tosses some flour at me. It lands in my lap. I laugh and wipe the flour stain from my jeans, catching a glimpse at the time. I quickly realize that I'm late for my date with Jeff.

"What's the matter?"

"I've got to go," I say. "I have a date with Jeff, remember?"

"You don't sound too excited."

"Oh," I huff. "You were probably right when you said I don't have time to date. Honestly, I suck in the relationship department anyway. Oh, well. What harm can *one* date do?"

Cole looks down at some flour that spilled on the floor. He kneels to wipe it up when a loud crash makes him jerk back to his feet. He glares at me as if hoping I had made the mysterious noise. I shake my head. My torso is frozen. I start having flashbacks of the night I was here all alone and kind of drunk.

Okay, I was completely drunk. But it had been a really tough first day.

"It's happening again," I mutter, covering my ears.

"What was that?" Cole stands up. His eyes are wide, and his fists are clenched. "I didn't hear anyone else come in. Did you?" He inches towards the hall.

"Stop," I blurt out. "You don't go searching for the *thing* making the freaky sounds." I point my finger at him. "Don't you watch horror films?"

"This isn't a horror movie, Poppy. It's a cooking school in a quiet town in Georgia. Nothing like that ever happens here."

"You don't know that," I whisper.

Another bang makes us both jump, but Cole opens the door leading into the hallway and begins looking for the source. My chest is pounding so hard that I feel like everyone on campus can hear it. I follow Cole with a worried look on my face. My gut tells me that this isn't a good idea.

"Shhh," he says, stopping outside one of the student kitchens. "I think it came from in there."

Through the tiny window on the door, I can't see a thing. The kitchen is pitch black.

"No one is in there," I point out.

"Someone *has* to be."

"Yeah," I gulp. "The ghost of pastries past." I grab his hand, hoping it will force him to leave before I have a panic attack and faint.

"But—"

"You heard what that guy Steve said when we first started," I mutter. "It's the ghost of Old Man Thomas." I glance around at the darkened hallway. The hairs on the back of my neck stand up when I mention the ghost story out loud.

"There's no such thing as ghosts." Cole says.

"Oh, yeah?" I retort. "Are you sure about that, because I've heard him banging around in there before. Now let's—"

"You've heard this noise before?" Cole asks. "When?"

"Yeah." I pull his hand again, but he's as solid as a rock. "I told you about it, remember? Our first night here?"

"That doesn't count," he argues. "You were tipsy."

My eyes go wide.

"Really? You want to debate this *now*?" I try dragging him towards the exit, but he won't budge. "Come on."

"Hold on," he argues. "Just let me—" The two of us hear the noise again. This time it's closer, and it startles me so much that I accidentally let out a yelp. The noise stops. All I hear is the sound of Cole breathing.

Cole glances at me before he carefully looks through the small window on the door again. I curiously take another peek too. I still don't see any light. Inside the room there's nothing but shadows.

One of the shadows looks as if it is moving. It creeps slowly towards us like a snake slithering to its prey. I gulp and jump back eyeing the door knob. If it starts turning on its own, that's it. I'll drive all the way back to Oregon screaming like a lunatic.

I don't have to plead with Cole to leave this time. His eyes are as wide as mine. He tightly grabs my arm and pulls me with him down the hall. Both of us almost trip over each other as we do. I feel the overwhelming urge to look behind me, but I stop myself. If I see a ghost glaring at me I won't be able to remove the image from my brain. I'll need meds to get a good night's sleep.

When we reach the night air, I take a huge breath. Cole paces the sidewalk with his hands on his hips. He scratches his brow and looks at me. I turn and start walking towards my apartment, hoping that a night with Jeff will help me forget all this.

"Stop," Cole instructs me. "Where are you going? We should report this."

"Report what?" I ask. "You sound *just* like Bree. We didn't see anything, unless you are counting Old Man Thomas who has returned from beyond the grave."

"That's a stupid story some student made up a long time ago," he states. He takes a few deep breaths. His expression looks sour like he's having an inner debate with himself. Probably the same one I had my first night here. *This proves that I'm not crazy.* "I heard someone. I know I did." Cole looks back at the building before he jogs up the steps again. He pulls on the door handles, but after dinner they all lock from the inside, so students can leave but no one can go back in.

"This never happened," I respond as he pulls the handles a second time. "Got it? I won't mention it if you won't mention it."

"Fine." He sighs and follows me across the quad. "If it makes you happy, I will believe in ghosts just this once."

CHAPTER SIX

────────

The smell of oatmeal raisin fills my nose when I open the front door to my apartment. I see Bree sitting on the couch with a hot mug of tea. A tiny dessert plate is on the coffee table displaying a few of her homemade cookies. Jeff is sitting across from her with his hands on his knees. His legs are long enough that they look a little squished between the sofa and the table.

"Look who decided to show," Bree says, smiling. If I could read minds I am almost positive she'd be shouting at me for setting her up for an awkward moment with Jeff.

"Sorry," I apologize. "How long have you been waiting?"

"Twenty minutes," Bree chimes in. "I told Jeff you were practicing batters on campus and probably lost track of time."

"Yes." I take a minute to catch my breath. "That's exactly what happened."

Bree studies my expression as she stands up with her mug and eagerly escapes to the kitchen. I smile at Jeff. He looks at my outfit and grins.

"You might want to change clothes for where we're going." He's wearing a simple pair of jeans and a blue T-shirt that brings out the color of his eyes.

"Why, where are we going?"

"You'll see." He shrugs, refusing to give anything else away.

"Right." I nod. "Give me a couple minutes." I head to my room and dig through my suitcase, grabbing a pair of slim jeans and a gray-striped tank top. I look in the mirror as I put on my diamond studs and let me hair fall past my shoulders in long, chocolate brown waves. I grab some high heels.

I feel more like myself wearing this.

"Okay," I say, entering the living area and grabbing Jeff's arm. "Let's go. Bye, Bree!"

"I won't wait up." She laughs from the kitchen.

"You look nice," Jeff responds as we walk to his car.

"Thanks."

He opens my door and quickly gets into the driver's seat. When he turns on the car, a CD begins playing death metal. Jeff blushes and turns the stereo off. I smile, mostly because I knew exactly what band he was listening to.

"So," I say, breaking the silence. "Not a huge fan of country music, huh?"

"If I were, I would definitely be in the right place," he replies.

"Yep." I glance out the window as he turns a corner, taking us into the little town square that I've only driven through once since I've been here. I usually spend the weekend grocery shopping and studying. I don't have time to do much else. I've even put off finding a few pieces of home décor to hang in my bedroom for a pop of color.

"So you're from Portland?"

"Yes," I answer. "And you?"

"Seattle."

"Right." I wrinkle my nose as we pull up to a gas station. There is a smirk on Jeff's face as he drives past the convenience store with a light bulb missing on the sign towards a bar surrounded by cars and motorbikes. My window is closed, but I can hear country music blasting inside.

"Told you that you were in the right place for some good ole country music," he jokes.

"What is this place?" I can hardly see through the windows because of all the neon beer signs.

"Nicky's."

I step out of the car, and immediately my heart starts racing.

"I've got to hand it to you, Jeff. You are full of surprises."

"Don't tell me you've never heard of Nicky's?" he says. "About half our class raves about it every Monday morning."

"I guess I'm always busy reading." I shrug and step carefully on the gravel path so I don't twist my ankles. Jeff walks slowly, assuming that I will too because of the shoes I'm wearing. I surprise him when I stroll up to the front door without any problems. I survived dancing pointe for half my life. High heels on a gravel road is no problem.

When Jeff opens the door a chime rings, but I can hardly hear it. Nicky's Bar looks exactly how I imagined it would. From outside I assumed it was one of those side of the highway stops with pool tables and men in leather drinking the night away. I assumed right. I follow Jeff to the bar, feeling out of my element. I focus on keeping my posture straight. I slouch when I'm nervous.

"Jeff," the barman says as we approach him. He's wearing an orange, flannel shirt, and it's tucked in so you can see just how far his beer belly extends. A thin strip of facial hair outlines his jaw, making him look like he's wearing a chin strap. The man holds out a hand, and Jeff shakes it like the two of them are old friends. "How are you, man?"

"Nice to see you, Nicky," Jeff answers. "Bring us two of the usual, will you?"

"Hey, man. You got it."

"Come here often?" I comment. Jeff rotates his stool so that he's facing the pool tables. He stretches out his arms and rests them on the counter.

"I spent a year in Ireland when I was twenty-five," he responds. He repositions his arms so that his bulky biceps are on full display. "Ever since then I *have* to know where my local pub is, no matter where I am."

"What did you do there for a whole year?"

He scoots a little closer to me. I bite the corner of my lip, staring briefly at his golden locks and the way they shine in the light. Jeff turns and looks at me. He chuckles and touches a strand of his hair.

"Do I have something on my face?" he teases.

"Your hair, actually." I squint, trying to look closer at a crusted piece of something hidden behind his ear. It looks like flour. Jeff automatically runs his fingers through his hair until he finds the leftover school assignment hiding in his mane.

"Oh." He wipes his hands on his shirt. "That's embarrassing."

"So." I change the subject. "Ireland, you say?"

"Oh, yes. I lived there for a while when I decided to backpack through Europe. I stopped in a little village where this old lady ran a book shop. She needed an assistant to do the bookkeeping, so I stayed for a while."

"Why did you leave?" I ask.

"Well." He turns his stool so it's facing the bar counter again. "My dad passed away, so I went home. Got a proper desk job and woke up one morning years later wondering what the hell I was doing."

"So you came here?"

Nicky hands the two of us a cold mug of beer. The froth on the top barely spills over onto the counter.

"Cheers." Jeff takes a sip and nods as Nicky places two baskets of fries in front of us. Fries are one of the many foods I've indulged in since I injured my back. Jeff watches me study the basket. I pick up a fry, impressed by how thick they are and how hot they are.

"Fresh out of the fryer," he comments, taking a bite.

I copy him but soon regret it when the heat sears my tongue. I pull the chunk of potato out of my mouth and blow on it until it's cool enough to taste. When I finally have the chance to try it I'm amazed that something this good came from *this* bar.

"That extra crunch it has—"

"Beer batter," Jeff says. "These are seriously some of the best beer battered fries I've had. Nicky's grandpa started making them with their leftover beer back in the day."

"Wow." I look behind the bar where the man called Nicky is wiping glasses with a clean rag. He briefly looks up and winks at me. "These are *really* good."

"Good enough for me to bring the bull out?" Nicky butts in. "We never get enough chicks in here who want to ride the bull."

"Don't push it, Nicky." Jeff laughs and takes another gulp of his beer. "He says that, yet they bring out the bull every weekend."

Nicky shrugs and chuckles to himself.

"Maybe I'll come back on a Saturday then," I respond.

"You heard her say it, man." Nicky nods and returns to tending his bar.

I can't imagine Bree in a place like this, riding a mechanical bull in front of drunken strangers. But there's still a lot I don't know about her, or Cole, or Jeff for that matter. I eat another fry, remembering my first greasy taste of them in college. My mom was very strict with me when it came to food. I guess that's why I always felt like it was Christmas when Grandma Liz came over to bake.

"You still haven't told me what your plans are when you graduate," I say, watching Jeff down his basket of fries like they might disappear any minute now.

"What are *your* plans?"

"Still deciding," I answer.

"I'm going to open a bagel shop." Jeff nods as he eats another fry in between breaths. "All kinds of bagels. And pastries, too."

"In Seattle?"

"Or Ireland." He chuckles. "We'll see what happens."

I take a tiny taste of my drink and slowly allow myself to relax. Inch by inch I work on my basket of fries, gradually forgetting about my incident with Cole. It feels good to let that all go for a night and pretend I'm not on the brink of failing my courses. I focus on the positive instead—the fact that I rocked those éclairs after class, and I'm sitting in a biker bar eating junk food with a guy who looks like he sleeps on the beach.

Before I have the chance to ask for a refill, Jeff's phone buzzes in his pocket. He pulls it out, and immediately his shoulders go tense. He turns slightly so that I can no longer see his lips. He clears his throat and reluctantly takes the call.

"Yeah," he says quietly. "Now? Really?" He takes a deep breath. "I'm kind of in the middle of something." He pauses for a couple minutes and rubs his forehead. "No," he mutters. "No. I don't want that. Okay, fine." He glances at me for a brief second. "Okay, I will. Bye."

"Is everything okay?" I ask. By the frazzled look in his eye, I know that it isn't.

"Yeah." He looks down at his empty basket. "It's just...something has come up and..."

"We need to get going," I finish.

My ex used to get that same look on his face when we would go out for Chinese. On more than one occasion he left suddenly because of some family emergency at his brother's food truck. Turns out our date nights kept landing on his *dudes only* poker night, and he was just too lazy to reschedule.

"Sorry."

"For what?" I make it easy for him by saying good-bye to Nicky and taking a handful of fries to go. "We came. We sat. We ate."

"I promise I'll make it up to you," Jeff replies.

That's what they always say.

"It's okay," I answer. "Thanks for the beer."

CHAPTER SEVEN

———

Cole looks a little tense as he takes his seat behind me. I know he's thinking about last night. I came home from my *half date* with Jeff and ended up eating most of Bree's oatmeal raisin cookies. I told her all about Jeff's sketchy phone call, all the while wanting to blurt out everything that Cole and I saw in the student kitchens. I promised Cole that we would forget about it, so I went to bed instead. I woke up about three times last night due to a very confused and very lost cricket in my room.

"Look who decided to show," Bree mutters. I look over my shoulder and see Jeff enter the classroom. He avoids looking in my direction. *Jerk.* Bree seems to be more offended than me that Jeff bailed on our date before it even got started. Maybe *she* should go out with him.

"Cut him some slack," I whisper. "Maybe there really was an emergency or something."

"Like what?" She shakes her head. "His roommate lost his key?"

"Listen up," Professor Sellers announces. "I have an important announcement to make." I focus my attention on the one teacher at CPA that I'm having a hard time liking. Not only did I sicken him with my lame attempt at pie making and nearly burn down his kitchen, but I called him Mr. Sellers once on accident because that's how we address all the other teachers. He reminded me that the proper way to address him was either *Professor* or *Chef*.

"This ought to be good," I whisper to Bree.

"Mr. Dixon wants me to inform you all of a little contest we are having this year."

"*Mr. Dixon*," I murmur. "Surely that's not the appropriate way to address the school's president."

Bree giggles.

"Perhaps you would like to make the announcement, Poppy." The professor looks right at me. I shake my head. "So sorry to interrupt your little conversation."

"No biggie," I snidely reply. He narrows his eyes and glares at me for a few seconds. He's trying to intimidate me, but it isn't going to work.

"As I was saying," he continues. "The school is putting on a contest, and all students are encouraged to enter. Entries will be made after the Christmas holiday."

"What kind of entries?" Georgina asks.

"Desserts." He smiles. "The best dessert will win, and that student will receive a position interning with the one and only *Jean Pierre*." The class breaks out in whispers. "Yes, that's right. The winning student will receive a coveted internship with one of the world's top pastry chefs in Paris."

"Paris?" I whisper. "I have always wanted to go there."

"What are the requirements for each entry?" Georgina asks. She's looking calm and collected compared to the students around her.

"One entry per student," Professor Sellers answers. "And you can submit anything that can be served as a dessert. No savory entries, please. The judges are looking for originality more than anything else. The recipe must be of your own creation. No team entries."

"Excellent," I hear Georgina say.

"What are you going to make?" I whisper to Bree. She shrugs and stares off into space.

Hardly anyone is paying attention when Professor Sellers starts explaining the differences between galettes and tarts. I find myself starting to daydream about Paris too. The cobblestone streets. The fresh farmers' markets. The authentic French food and an excuse to eat carbs three times a day. I have to win that contest. It will prove to everyone and to myself that I *do* belong here, and I *am* a good chef.

Not to mention winning would be the perfect payback for Georgina.

"Red velvet," Bree mutters.

"Huh?"

"I think maybe I'll do a red velvet layered cake," she says.

"Well, you are the best cake maker here." I am happy for her, but I am also jealous, because I know she will be a top contender. I glance over at Georgina who is taking notes. I am sure she already has her entry perfectly planned out in her head.

And the judges' phone numbers on speed dial.

I doodle on my notepad and feel like it has only been minutes when Professor Sellers concludes his lecture and leaves us to do our assignment for the day. We've been tasked with making a simple fruit tart with ingredients of our choice, but this time we have to calculate our own nutrition facts.

"Remember," Professor Sellers says as he passes my desk. "There is such a thing as too sweet."

I nod and accept his advice even though inside I'm cursing at him.

"Sounds like my last boyfriend," Bree jokes.

"So red velvet, huh?" I turn to her and close my notebook. "Isn't that a southern thing? It will have to be *really* good to win."

"I have an old school recipe with beet juice and everything," she comments. "I only break it out for special occasions, because it's *amazing*."

"Wow."

"What about you?" she asks. "What are you going to submit?"

I've been wondering the same thing myself. My mind is moving at a million miles a minute trying to decide. I want to perfect something that takes a lot of skill. If I do that, the judges will know that I mean business. I am not just an average woman about to turn thirty who thinks that Betty Crocker counts as being made from scratch because you have to mix it.

"What do you think of a napoleon?"

"Whoa." Her eyes go wide. "Aren't those kind of tricky to make?"

"But they're good."

"There's a ton of ways to mess it up," she goes on. "First there's the consistency of the cream, and then there's the puff pastry that can go soggy on you. Not to mention you have to make the design on top look artistic and professional, and—"

"Okay," I interrupt. "I get it. It's risky, and I've never made one before."

"You better get practicing."

I was afraid she might say that.

"I'm going to have my serving platter handmade and flown in from New York City," I hear Georgina say. She is talking to one of her friends as she cuts kiwis. She's purposely talking loud enough for the entire classroom to hear. Georgina lifts her chin and continues to talk about how she has this secret family recipe that has won all kinds of awards in the past. She thinks she's the winner already.

"I don't care who wins," Bree mutters under her breath. "As long as someone beats *her*."

I laugh and get to work on my tart. I start by mixing my crust, but I stop when the strong scent of cologne fills my nose. I sniff my strawberries again to make sure I'm not going crazy. A hand touches my shoulder, and makes my chest start pounding.

"Hey, Poppy," Jeff says.

"Oh, hey." I carry on with my tart like nothing is wrong.

"About last night," he begins. "I really am sorry about how things played out."

"Don't worry about it," I respond.

He grins. He must have thought I would put up a fuss. Scold him, maybe? Instead I do what I usually do when guys act lame. I try to make them jealous.

"I am a man of my word. I'll make it up to you."

"Actually," I respond. "I am not sure I'll have time now with this contest coming up. Cole and I are going to be in here practicing every night and weekend I suspect."

"Oh." Jeff looks surprised. He folds his arms. I look up at him and his ice blue eyes glimmer in the light.

"He's a good tutor." I sigh.

"Cole?" he repeats.

I look back at Cole and wait for him to make eye contact. When he does I wink at him for Jeff to see. Cole stares at me looking confused before shaking his head.

"Maybe after midterms?"

"Sure," he replies. "Midterms."

I nod.

As he grins and walks away, I hear Bree giggle. She glares at me like I'm insane for letting Jeff get off that easy.

"If he's not your type just tell him," she whispers. "Otherwise, make him buy you a nice steak dinner."

"I don't know if I like him like that or not," I admit. "It's complicated."

"Are you sure?" Bree glances back at him with a twinkle in her eye. She tosses her strawberry blonde locks over her shoulder. "He stinks at first impressions, but I hear he drinks as much coffee as you do."

"Hang on." I raise my eyebrows. "Weren't you the one who called him a jerk earlier?"

"I can't help it. I'm unusually bitter when it comes to flaky men. He's a jerk for running off like he did, but that doesn't mean you have to turn him away." She glances over her shoulder at Georgina who is forming her tart in her specialized tart pan.

"Oh." I place a hand on my chest and sport a wide grin. "I see what you're doing. You *want* me to lead Jeff on just long enough to drive Georgina crazy."

Bree looks away and gets back to slicing peaches. She chooses a small bowl and begins measuring ingredients to mix her glaze. She arranges her fruit on her cutting board in the shape of her tart. She studies the design before shaking her head and changing it.

"So," she breathes. "It's the least you could do to get her back for what she did to you."

"This contest will take care of that," I say quietly. "Can you imagine the look on her face if *I* won?" Bree pauses for a minute and nods in agreement.

I take a deep breath, realizing that if I want to win I will have to give up all of my free time.

All of it.

* * *

I bite the bullet and stay after my evening class with Miss Chester to begin practicing the art of napoleons. Cole promised his roommate that he would make dinner, so he said he would meet me later if I needed him. I reminded him that I wasn't planning on using an oven, so he had the night off.

Miss Chester cleans up her station as I turn my focus to napoleons. I look at a few pictures of this tasty dessert on my laptop for inspiration. There are so many things I have to figure out.

Do I want to use fruit?

Do I want to use chocolate?

Do I want to make a traditional vanilla napoleon or come up with my own concoction?

"Are you sure you don't want my help?" Miss Chester asks before leaving me by myself. Despite the rumors circulating about me among the staff, Miss Chester's opinion of me hasn't seemed to change. She is a patient middle-aged woman. She's short, petite, and light on her feet. She also whips together most of the recipes in my school booklet by heart. She traveled the world working for a company that organizes chocolate shows. I had no idea that things like that even existed until she shared her story with the class. Miss Chester went from event planning to entering her own confections in competitions, eventually winning a national award for her mint chocolate bonbon.

"Ask me in a week or two," I reply. "I want to try and figure it out on my own first."

"I'm rooting for you, Poppy." She takes off her glasses and picks up her purse. "You don't have as much experience as the other students but you are more creative than most."

"Thanks, Miss Chester."

"Class is over. Call me Mel." She smiles and glances at the pictures of napoleons on my laptop on her way out. "Ballsy choice."

"I am hoping it will show the judges that I belong here."

"As long as *you* believe it." She glances at the time. "Ah, I need to get home to Norman."

"So you *are* married?" I ask, feeling way more comfortable asking her personal questions that any of the other teachers. "Some of us have wondered that since you hardly ever bring up your personal life. On second thought, none of the teachers really do."

"Norman is my cat," she laughs. "And as for the lower level teachers, all you need to know is that Mr. Harris is an old grump with a hot temper, Mr. Sellers has been extra snide since his messy divorce, and *I* spend all my free time writing a baking blog."

"Really? I would never guess that you were a blogger. Do you write as well as you bake?"

"Probably not," she responds. "Oye, that sounds braggy, doesn't it? Yep. I better get going. Norman gets pissy if I'm not home by dinnertime."

She takes her time shutting the door behind her. It creaks slightly as it closes, and instantly I am left alone with my thoughts. I wander through the pantry and grab a few ingredients for my dough. I decide to start with the basics and make a classic napoleon with vanilla custard filling and cocoa dusted on top. I will perfect a pretty design later. Right now, all I care about is taste.

"Light and fluffy," I repeat out loud as I form my dough. "Light and fluffy."

I knead enough dough to make a few different flavors before setting it in the fridge to rest. I will have to leave the dough here overnight. Tomorrow I will know just how light and fluffy I made it. I take a deep breath and begin cleaning up my station.

I stop when the room becomes eerily silent. I can hear my heart pounding, and my thoughts start spinning out of control. I think back to the last time I was here after hours. I got so anxious that I almost passed out. I force myself to wipe the counter so I can leave.

As soon as I do, I hear it.

The noise.

A loud bang sounds from the kitchens across the hall. A horrified squeak forces its way out of my mouth as I jump. I swallow the lump in my throat and grab my things. I don't want to be here anymore. I don't know what's going on in this building once the sun goes down, but I don't want to stay and find out.

My legs feel like blocks of concrete as I walk out of the classroom. I have to force myself to move faster and avoid looking behind me down the dark hallway. The banging noise haunts my memories. I hear it clanging around in my brain, and I can't tell if what I am hearing is real or not anymore. My forehead starts to sweat, and my stomach is churning. I feel dizzy again like before. I focus on the front door ahead of me. All I want to do is breathe in the hot, Georgian air. If I can make it that far then everything will be fine.

"Poppy?"

The voice startles me, and I let out a scream. I turn around and see Professor Sellers with his arms folded and his lips curled. He's studying my expression with a curious look on his face. His eyes dart around the hall.

I gulp.

"Professor," I say quietly.

"What are you doing here?" he quickly asks me.

"Practicing for the contest. Napoleons." I place a hand on my pounding chest. "I wasn't using the ovens, I swear."

"Napoleons?" he repeats. "Those are pretty difficult."

"So I've heard." I shrug, digging my nails into my skin. Why is he staring at me like that? I just want to go back to my apartment and share a chocolate croissant with the psychotic cricket living in my room. *Anything* is better than this. I can't stomach the awkwardness anymore. "See you tomorrow." I turn and bolt for the door.

If Professor Sellers said anything else, I didn't hear it. My mind is too busy screaming *get out of here!*

CHAPTER EIGHT

———

I'm uneasy as I slip into Professor Sellers' class. I slump my shoulders and sit at my station anxious to get this class over with. Bree takes her notebook out of her book bag with a smile on her face. I wanted to tell her about last night, but she wasn't home when I burst through the door to our apartment.

"Are you going to tell me where you were last night?" I ask her quietly.

"I went out with Tessa and Jill next door to celebrate. I was chosen for a special assignment." Her face is glowing. "The student bakery is short-staffed, and Mr. Harris picked me to start my rotations early. Wonderful, isn't it?"

"If you like getting up at 3 a.m."

"Poppy," she whines. "I must be building a noteworthy reputation if he thought of me first. I mean, he could have asked Georgina, but he didn't."

"True."

"Poppy Peters," Professor Sellers announces. "You are wanted in Mr. Dixon's office."

President Dixon.

My face feels abnormally hot, and Cole stares at me as I exit the classroom. I walk outside and towards the adjacent building where the president's office is. I wipe the sweat from my cheeks when I jog down the steps and into the blaring sun. My heart rate increases as I near the president's building. *What did I do this time?*

A cool breeze blasts across my face when I open the door to the adjacent building. The air conditioning in here works much better than in the kitchens. I count my steps as I walk to the president's office. I pass an empty reception desk and a small waiting area with a tan sofa and two leather chairs. The office door is open, and I can hear President Dixon typing on his computer. My shoes make squeaking noises as I walk closer. The typing stops.

"Poppy Peters?" Mr. Dixon asks, peeking around the corner of his desk.

"That's me."

"Come on in and have a seat," he instructs.

I sit down and place a hand on my churning stomach. I glance around his office and spot a group photo of him, a woman, and three younger women next to his screen. I assume that they are his family. His desk is made of dark oak. The wood matches a giant bookshelf behind him that spans the length of the wall. The walls that can be seen are painted a light peachy color. It contrasts with a dark green plant sitting in a pot near the door. I can't tell if it's real or just for decoration.

On his desk there is a half-eaten ham sandwich that has been cut in half very neatly. Not a single crumb is sitting on the plate and next to Mr. Dixon's hand is a perfectly folded napkin. A ham sandwich is an interesting choice of snack for the president of a cooking school.

"What is this about?" I ask, glancing down at his sandwich. He catches me looking at it and grins.

"Old habit," he comments. "In my younger years I was a train conductor. The work is harder than most people would expect. My wife always sent me off for the day with enough ham sandwiches to last me a full twelve hours or more. We didn't have the money for anything fancy back then. Just plain white bread with the generic, sale-price ham." He pushes aside the plate. "But that's beside the point."

Mr. Dixon clasps his hands together and places them on his neatly organized desk. He has a serious look on his face. He narrows his eyes when he looks at me, causing a cascade of wrinkles to appear on his forehead. I hear him take a deep breath before he opens his mouth.

My pinky finger twitches. I think about my first day here at Calle Pastry Academy, my little oven incident on day two, and the multiple run-ins I have had with the ghost of Old Man Thomas. I have no idea which of these things he's going to bring up. Maybe he will bring up all three?

"Last night," he begins. My shoulders shudder. Last night was one of those nights that is going to keep me from sleeping for a while. "A package of expensive black truffles was stolen from the student kitchens."

"Black truffles?"

"Yes," he goes on. "Essentially, they are mushrooms used in upscale, savory dishes. They are very pricey, and good quality isn't always easy to come by. I finally found a trusted source and purchased a package to use to cater the Governor's Ball. It is a V.I.P. event that this school has been involved in for years."

"Oh," I gasp. "Well, that's terrible."

"Yes, it's most terrible. The entire package cost the school $20,000. We are expecting double the guests this year now that the mayor of Birmingham has also accepted our invitation."

I nearly choke when he tells me how much the truffles cost. Never in a million years did I think this is what he was going to say to me. *Stolen mushrooms.* He keeps looking at me, and I immediately realize why I am here. My eyes go wide.

"You think *I* had something to do with it?" The worst thing I've ever stolen was a tube of lip gloss, and I was seven-years-old.

"Professor Sellers informed me that you were in the building after hours last night," he responds. "And you were alone."

"Yeah, but—"

"So you *were* in the building," he says.

"I was practicing my dessert for the contest," I exclaim. "I didn't steal anything. Search my apartment. Search my book bag." I look down at my pockets and do my best to turn them inside out. "See. All *empty.*"

"I am very sorry, Poppy." He looks down and shakes his head. "At the moment, you are the only suspect. Yesterday afternoon, after classes ended, the truffles were locked in a storage cupboard."

"What?" I gasp. "What about Professor Sellers? He was wandering the halls after hours. Why isn't he a suspect?" A sharp pain is starting to build behind my eyes like a stress migraine is beginning to take shape.

"Stuart said he was working late in his office. Besides, he's a highly esteemed staff member here. I trust the folks I hire." President Dixon takes a deep breath, and hangs his head. "This isn't easy for me, Miss Peters. The last thing I want to do is interrupt your future plans." He pauses again and sighs. The president's eyes go soft as he glances at the family photo on his desk. "I am very sorry to have to do this, but if the thief isn't caught I will have no choice but to expel you."

"No," I protest. "You can't do this." I feel tears forming. They run down my cheeks as I stand up to leave.

"Now, wait. I have a team of investigators looking into it. If you have nothing to hide, your name should be cleared in no time."

"Okay," I say quietly. I don't know what else to do but run back to Professor Sellers' class and give him an earful. "What am I supposed to do until then?"

Mr. Dixon scratches the side of his cleanly shaven chin, and looks again at his prized picture on his desk. He lightly touches it and then looks back at me.

"Look, Poppy, you seem like a nice, reasonable young lady but rules are rules."

"Please," I exclaim. "You can't pull me out of classes now. Not when I've come so far. Please, sir!"

"Okay," he exhales, tapping his fingers on the desk. "I suppose if it were one of my daughters, I would hope that they would be given a fair chance to succeed. I will allow you to stay in your classes, *but* only if you promise to stay out of trouble."

"Yes, President Dixon."

"I sure do hope you aren't fibbing, Miss Peters. I would hate to see my students behave this way."

"I promise," I assure him. "My name will be cleared. I didn't steal anything."

"Good." He clears his throat. "Because aside from jail time, you would owe the school $20,000 plus damages."

His words make my blood go cold. I don't have that kind of money, and I doubt that I could get that kind of money anytime soon. I don't even have a job at the moment. I wipe away more tears as I exit the building and head back to class. I can't bring myself to step back inside. I would rather jump into my car and start driving until the sun goes down. I can't believe Professor Sellers ratted me out for something that *he* probably did.

I'm calling him Stuart from now on.

I lean against the wall outside the classroom and try to calm myself down. I fold my arms and think back to last night. There must be some way that I can clear my name. I look up when the door creaks open. Cole steps out. His feet move towards the restrooms until he sees me half crying in the hallway.

"Poppy," he says. "What happened?"

"That dirty little rat," I mutter. "Remember those noises we heard when we stayed late to—"

"I thought we agreed never to bring that up." He looks up and down the hallway like someone might be listening to our conversation.

"Last night I stayed late and made a few overnight batters for my dessert entry." I pause and sniffle. "I heard those noises again."

"Poppy," he says, taking my hand. "Please tell me you didn't roam the halls by yourself."

"Of course not," I protest. "I bolted. But I ran into Professor Sellers."

"Professor Sellers?" He speaks softly as if talking at a normal volume might hurt my feelings.

"Yes, *Professor Sellers*." I smack his arm.

"Then what did the president want?"

"*Also* last night," I gulp. "Something was stolen—a $20,000 package of black truffles, and guess who the only suspect is right now?"

"No way," Cole responds. "What about—"

"He has an alibi, I guess." I interrupt him because I am tired of hearing that man's name. He should be the one being investigated, not me. "Cole, if the police don't figure out who the thief is, I will be expelled."

Cole's eyes widen. He shakes his head and clenches his jaw.

"No," he disagrees. "I won't let that happen."

"It's not for you to decide," I mutter.

"Then we'll prove that you're not the thief." He takes a step back and looks at me until I stop frowning. "Now, go home and take a nap. I'll catch you up on today's class later."

I sigh and wipe my runny nose on my sleeve.

"Fine. I doubt that *Mr. Sellers* is expecting me back anyways. At all."

"Meet me here after dark," Cole says.

"Are you crazy?" My heart starts racing just thinking about what goes on in this building when the sun goes down.

"Maybe?" He chuckles. "But do you know a better way to clear you name?"

* * *

I hear the front door slam, and it rouses me from a deep sleep. I came back to my apartment and took a nap, letting the subtle chirps of the cricket in my room lull me to sleep. I hear Bree in the kitchen shuffling pots and pans before she heads towards my room.

"Poppy?" She says. "Poppy, are you here?"

"I'm in my room," I shout. I sit up and see her standing in the doorway with her hands on her hips.

"Please tell me it's not true." She folds her arms and plays with the charm on her silver necklace. "They can't expel you. It's...outrageous!"

"Bree, I'm not expelled."

"Then why was Georgina saying that you were going to be expelled after class today?"

"Georgina said that?" Clearly, I was not the first to know about the missing truffles. "Well, maybe she's assuming that because I was called into the president's office."

"Yes," Bree replies. "Why were you called into the office? You didn't do anything wrong."

"The president of our school disagrees." I rub my eyes, trying to fully wake myself up before I get into more details. On my short walk home I debated whether or not to tell her the truth about the truffles. She nearly had a meltdown after Georgina sabotaged my oven. "The bottom line is that I haven't been expelled, and Cole has a plan to clear my name. At least, I hope he does."

"What?" Her cheeks start turning red, and her lips purse together like she's forcing herself not to shout what she really thinks.

"Sorry." I change the tone of my voice so it sounds more upbeat. "It was nothing to get excited about. Just a misunderstanding—that's all." She nods and makes eye contact until I nod reassuringly.

"Uh-huh." She tucks a strand of strawberry blonde hair behind her ear. "Well, I'll be in the kitchen if you want to talk about it. Oh, and Miss Chester cancelled our afternoon classes to give us time to practice our dessert entries. I guess a lot of students are really freaking out about it."

"It's Paris." I take a deep breath. "That's a huge prize to win."

"Or to lose," she adds.

As soon as I hear her back in the kitchen I collapse back onto my pillow. I feel like I'm back where I started on day one. Cole better have a solid plan, because he's my only hope. It's like I'm in the middle of a reality baking show, and I keep getting sent to the chopping block. *By myself.*

* * *

The sky is dark, and the air is crisp. I have goose bumps on my arms as I wait for Cole to show up. I have no idea how he plans on breaking into our school building, and I'm not sure if I want to find out. My heart is pounding from all the espressos I drank when I finally got up from my nap. I couldn't stop thinking long enough to let myself sleep any longer.

I stand next to a tree, hoping its shadow will be enough to keep me hidden from any psychopaths that might be roaming around campus. There is an eerie, absolute silence and dark shapes that move along the sidewalks as the wind blows. It's only the waving tree branches, but it still gives me the creeps.

The door to the building slowly opens. I stand stiff in my hiding spot until a familiar face peeks outside. It's Cole, and he is already inside the building waiting. I step into the moonlight so he can see me. As soon as he does, he waves his hand. I run to the doors as if something might snatch my leg if I don't move fast enough. Cole pulls me inside the building and quickly shuts the door. It makes a clicking noise when it closes. He hands me my own flashlight and nudges me forward.

"How did you get inside?" I whisper.

"I came just before they lock the doors," he responds. "I read ahead for our kitchen management class and hid in the bathrooms when security came and did a sweep a while ago."

"Dang." I gulp. "So what's the plan?"

"Break into Professor Sellers' office," he says casually. I roll my eyes, but I suppose deep down I know it's the only lead we have. That man has to be the thief. And if he isn't the truffle thief, he's hiding something.

"You make it sound so simple."

"I don't know how to pick a lock, but how hard can it be?" Cole whispers back. "*Do you*?" He chuckles to himself, expecting me to say no. I grin and begin walking down the main level hallway.

"It depends on the lock," I say quietly. I shine my light close to Cole and see that he looks surprised. "What? You think *every* girl that goes to ballet school wears pink and watches dance movies?"

"I'm not even going to ask." He walks next to me pointing his flashlight down at the floor. We pass our usual classroom. I cringe as I think about all the times I've heard those freakish noises. If it happens tonight, I don't know if I will be able to compose myself.

The professor's office isn't far from the kitchens. As we pass the locked kitchen where Cole and I had attempted to investigate the source of the mysterious sounds, my stomach churns. My gut tells me that we shouldn't be here. I remind myself that there's no other way to make sure my name is cleared. I don't want to be labeled a thief and kicked out of the one place I thought could change everything for me.

"Right over here," Cole whispers.

We come to the door to the professor's office. Cole tries the door knob. I watch anxiously, hoping we will get lucky. Cole frowns. The door is locked.

"Let me try," I sigh. I examine the doorknob and find that the lock is a fairly easy one to pick. "We lucked out that this is a very old building. Give me your wallet." Cole raises his eyebrows. "Relax, I just need one of your credit cards."

"Do you prefer Visa or American Express?"

I put my hands on my hips. Cole quickly pulls out a random card and hands it to me. I yank at the door handle and try to push down the lock. It takes me a few tries, but the door finally creaks open. Cole looks impressed as the door swings in, revealing our professor's tidy office.

"Sometimes, when I was in college, I would come home after curfew," I say. "My roommates always locked me out."

"Sure," he teases.

We step into the Professor Sellers' office, and I am not surprised that everything is perfectly organized in file folders and on shelves with labels. I start with his desk, running my fingers over his keyboard and reading a few of the sticky notes stuck to his monitor.

Order more bread flour.

Pay phone bill.

Out of toilet paper.

I wrinkle my nose.

"Find anything?" Cole asks. He continues skimming through the professor's files.

"No, unless running out of toilet paper counts as something suspicious."

"T-M-I," he mutters. "There's nothing over here. Just class schedules and paperwork."

"Well, there has to be *something* that might give us a clue. See if you can figure out where he lives or something. He wouldn't leave the truffles sitting in his office overnight." I shake my head. "Cole, I don't want to be expelled. I *know* Professor Sellers has something to do with this. I mean for starters, he hates me."

"He doesn't *hate* you, Poppy."

"Okay, well I am definitely not his favorite."

"That's not a bad thing," Cole responds. "Trust me." He opens a few desk drawers and skims through a few more papers. "Georgina and her flying monkeys aren't going to win the dessert contest. They aren't creative enough to pull it off."

"I don't know," I argue. "I overheard her saying that she's using a custom-made serving platter."

"Ooooo," Cole chants. "I forgot that fancy dishes make food taste better."

"Shut up," I mutter. I slump my shoulders but immediately catch myself doing it. We just violated a ton of school rules for nothing. We aren't going to find anything in here. I rub my forehead, starting to feel even more anxious. My palms are clammy, and my chest feels like it's carrying a ten-pound sponge cake.

Cole and I are interrupted by a shrieking noise.

I fall against the desk, nearly hitting my head on a jagged edge. The loud scream came from the kitchens. I look at Cole. His eyes are wide, and his face is going pale. I can tell he's frozen in place just like me, because he hasn't taken a breath yet.

"Did you?" I gasp. My voice is shaky, and I was barely able to force the words out of my mouth.

"Yeah," he whispers.

We quickly move closer to each other before deciding what to do next. I really hope a human didn't make that sound and that it was just a really hairy cat getting into the ventilation system.

"Should we check it out?" I suggest.

Cole nods as he slowly pushes the door aside and leads the way. I instinctively grab his hand. Our fingers intertwine perfectly as we walk slowly towards the kitchens. I gulp. I can hear myself breathing.

Cole stops suddenly.

The door to one of the student kitchens is open.

Light is flooding through the doorway, and Cole looks back at me.

"I'm going in this time," he whispers. "You stay here and keep watch." Before I can take a breath, I hear the sound of banging pots and pans. It sparks a feeling of terror deep down in my gut. Cole stands up straight. His wide shoulders are flexed, and his fists are clenched.

A part of me is curious, but a part of me is terrified.

I nod without thinking.

"No," I answer, blinking repeatedly in order to clear my thoughts. "You're not leaving me here by myself. No. I'm going in with you."

I follow Cole into the kitchen. My eyes instantly dart from the body on the floor to the open back door leading to the Dumpsters. The kitchen is a mess with pots and pans strewn all over the place. It looks like Cole and I walked in after a food fight. *A deadly food fight.* Baking ingredients are all over the floor. They make clouds of dust with every step we take.

I look at the motionless body on the floor and gasp when I realize it is Professor Sellers. I rush to his side. He isn't breathing as far as I can see. I feel for a pulse, but I can't find one. I start to panic, slapping his face hoping it will work. It doesn't.

"Is he dead?" Cole asks, afraid of the answer.

I swallow the lump in my throat.

"Call an ambulance!" I shout. I don't know what else to do. Nothing like this has ever happened to me before. I watch Cole as he immediately pulls out his cell phone and dials 911. His fingers fumble over the keys. His voice is low and quiet as he asks for an ambulance. His face is still pale. He might be in shock.

I force myself to be the calm one.

I take a deep breath and try again to wake up Professor Sellers. There is a bruise forming on his forehead as if he was hit over the head with something hard. The bruise is a distinct shape, but staring at his face too long creeps me out. I shake his shoulders, staring at the splotches of flour all over his clothes. There is so much of it that it couldn't have been an accident. He must have walked in on someone.

My eyes dart down to his hands. One is open, and one hand is clenched around something. I swallow hard as I touch the professor's palm and find a crumpled piece of paper. Sirens ring through the night. I shove the piece of paper into my pocket and join Cole near the back door. The minute we see lights flashing outside, we wave our arms. The ambulance driver sees us and comes speeding onto the sidewalk.

"Over here," Cole instructs them. The color in his face is starting to come back.

A paramedic races to Professor Sellers and shakes his head as he feels for a pulse. Two more paramedics nudge us aside. Cole and I take a few steps back until we are outside waiting for the bad news. A few students are up and are walking towards the flashing lights from their dorms. I gulp and glance at Cole.

"I feel sick," I mutter. "Maybe we should go?"

"Cops," he replies.

"What?"

"Don't you hear that? There are more sirens. The cops will be here any minute."

"Let's go," I respond. *I can't hang around here any longer. I am in enough trouble as it is.*

"You do know that no matter where you go, the cops will pull us in for questioning," he states.

"Yep." I take a few more calming breaths, but my head starts to spin.

I think about the scream.

The body.

Getting kicked out of Calle Pastry Academy for being too curious.

Suddenly, I'm having a hard time breathing.

"Poppy," Cole says. "Poppy!"

But the more he says my name the less and less I hear it. Everything seems fuzzy, and my eyelids feel like heavy gallons of cookie dough ice cream. I feel myself falling. I don't know if I'm hitting the ground or if someone caught me because everything goes black before I have the chance to find out.

CHAPTER NINE

"Poppy."

I hear voices.

"Poppy, are you okay?"

I open my eyes slowly. Bree is sitting next to me with a worried look on her face. She feels my forehead and reaches for a glass of water sitting on the coffee table. I look around and realize I'm back in my apartment. I am lying on the couch with my hands clasped neatly on my stomach. I sit up, rubbing my cheeks. They are warm, and I am starting to remember bits and pieces of what happened earlier. I glance outside and see that it's still dark.

"Poppy?"

I am relieved to hear Cole's voice.

"Cole," I say. "What happened?"

"You passed out," he replies. "I brought you straight here."

The image of Professor Sellers, cold and lifeless on the kitchen floor, seems like a distant memory. I lie to myself and picture that moment as nothing but a ludicrous nightmare, but I know in my heart that it's not. I also know that if I don't get to the bottom of this right away, *I* or anyone else on campus could be next.

"What's going on out there?" Bree asks. She stands up and walks into the kitchen. She returns with a small plate of lemon bars dusted with confectioner's sugar.

"Lemon bars?" I mutter. "What time is it? Like 4 a.m.?"

"It's not *that* late," Cole blurts out, grabbing a bar. Bree smiles as she watches Cole take a bite of her lemony dessert. She hands him a napkin to wipe his face.

"What do you think?" she asks.

"These are *really* good," Cole admits.

"Award-winning good?" She waits anxiously for him to answer.

"I thought you were entering your red velvet cake in the contest?" I frown. I was looking forward to tasting her practice cakes.

"I'm starting to second guess myself," Bree mutters, looking down at the floor.

"What?" I respond.

"And," she adds. "I might have overheard someone else in our class who is making the same thing as me."

"Who?" Cole asks. "I'll crush him."

Bree smiles. Her cheeks go rosy as she sets her plate of lemon bars on the coffee table.

"It doesn't matter," she answers. "What matters is that Poppy is okay."

"Yeah, I think so." I try standing, but my legs are a little wobbly.

"Good." Bree looks at me and Cole with her hands on her curvy hips. "So, are you two going to tell me what's going on? Don't say it's nothing, because I know there is something you are not telling me."

"Well," I sigh. I glance at Cole. He stares at me. I know he's trying to tell me something with his facial expressions, but I don't catch on. I have no clue what he wants me to say. Bree looks in Cole's direction.

"I knew it," she says, giggling. "You two were off fooling around, weren't you?"

"What do you mean, exactly?" I respond.

Her face turns red. She turns away from Cole, so she's looking at me only.

"You know," she mutters. "You two are…"

"What?"

"For heaven's sake, Poppy, don't make me say it." Bree stamps her foot. "If you guys are friends with benefits just say so. We are all adults here."

My eyes go wide. The thought of me and Cole together sends my heart racing, but I quickly shake my head. I have much more pressing things on my plate right now than homework and silly crushes.

"No," I respond. "We're not…"

"She's right," Cole chimes in. "We aren't…you know."

"Okay," Bree says, looking suspicious. "Then what were you doing out so late?"

"What do you think?" I ask Cole.

"Once we tell her, she's part of it." Cole takes a deep breath and scratches his chin.

"Part of what?" Bree asks.

I debate whether or not to say anything. I don't want my problems to get in her way. Bree is one of the best chefs in our class. She's a perfectionist when it comes to sweets, and I've never met anyone who has baked as many chocolate chip cookies as she has.

"Bree, you know how I was practicing for the contest the other night?"

"Napoleons," she says. "Let me guess. They didn't turn out? Honey, I told you they were difficult."

"Well, apparently I was the only student in the building that night and…" I look up at Cole. "That's the night that a $20,000 package of black truffles was stolen from the student kitchens. Mr. Dixon thinks it was me. If my name isn't cleared soon, I'll be expelled."

"No," she gasps. "I knew you were lying. You should have just told me the truth."

"It gets worse," Cole adds. He looks at me. "I'm sorry, Poppy. I'm sorry that I suggested we go snooping in the first place. This is all because of me."

"It wasn't your fault." I stand up and look out the window at the night sky.

"Poppy," Bree scolds me. "Tell me what happened tonight."

"The afternoon the black truffles were stolen, there was another person in the building. But Mr. Dixon said *he* wasn't being considered a suspect." I frown. "It was Professor Sellers." I pause to wait for her reaction. She patiently waits for me to continue, though a look of distaste spreads across her face.

"So," Cole continues. "*I* suggested that we try to clear her name, starting by snooping around Professor Sellers' office. That's what we were doing tonight. I thought that we might find a clue or something linking him to the theft." He pauses to take a deep breath. "While we were in his office we heard…a scream. That's when we found the professor on the floor in one of the student kitchens. He was dead."

"Dead?" Bree quietly repeats. She looks at me as if waiting for me to say *April fools*. Cole and I stay silent as she swallows the information. I nervously tap my foot and pick at my nails, waiting for tears. For her to start yelling. Crying. Acting hysterical. Something.

She opens her mouth.

"Well, if he's dead then of course he was involved," she responds. "I'll bet you that whoever murdered him is the thief."

Cole and I look at each other.

"Um…" I am at a loss for words.

"Well," Bree goes on. "What did you see? Tell me everything. Did you see anybody else? Did you hear the killer escape?"

"You did hear what I just said, right? One of our teachers is dead. Are you sure that you are feeling alright?" Cole says looking at Bree.

"Oh, please." She laughs. "I live alone with three cats, and I spend my weekends making my own chocolate molds. This is the most exciting thing that has *ever* happened to me."

I try not to laugh with her.

"So you're not freaked out?" I ask.

"You two aren't the murderers, are you?"

"Gosh *no*," I blurt out. "How could you even ask that?"

"Yeah," Cole adds. "I'm insulted."

"Then it looks like we have a mystery to solve," Bree responds. "And fast—before you two are pulled into the police station for questioning."

"Look at you," I say. "I never thought my roomie would turn out to be a Nancy Drew enthusiast."

"Sherlock Holmes," she corrects me. "I've never actually read *Nancy Drew*."

"That makes two of us," I say.

Cole stares at us like we're crazy.

"Back to the murder," Bree says casually. "Tell me everything you saw."

I take a deep breath and look down at my pocket. My fingers reach for the piece of paper that was in the professor's hand. I quickly open it, careful not to damage the paper. A name is written on it.

"Shurbin Farms?" I say out loud. Bree turns to look at me.

"We buy our peaches from them," Bree says.

"How do you know that?" I ask.

"The student bakery. I was asked to start my rotations early, remember?"

"Oh, right," I respond. The words are written by hand, probably in Professor Sellers' handwriting.

"Where did you get that?" Cole asks, staring at the crumpled piece of paper.

"It was in the professor's hand," I answer. "I put it in my pocket. I don't know why I did that."

"It's a clue." Bree jumps up and grabs a notebook and pen. "Anything else?"

"Well, the kitchen was covered in flour?" Cole adds.

"And the professor had a bruise on his head like he was knocked out with something heavy." I watch Bree scribble everything down.

"Kitchen equipment?" she suggests.

"Probably." Cole finally sits down and allows himself to relax a little. "I wonder if he walked in on..." Cole looks at me, and this time I understand what he's thinking. He makes the same face he did the night we heard the ghost of *Old Man Thomas*.

"He wasn't murdered by a ghost," I reassure him.

"You better hope not or else the killer will never be caught."

"Hold on," Bree interjects. "Am I missing something?"

"Yeah," I gulp. "That story about how the ghost of Old Man Thomas still haunts the kitchens. It's true. Cole and I heard the banging around one night, and when we went to see what it was no one was there."

Cole looks down like he would rather not talk about it.

"Ghost of Old Man Thomas," Bree mutters. "That's absurd."

"Then what do *you* think happened?" Cole waits for her to come up with something better.

"There's always an explanation. And if there really is a ghost hanging around the student kitchens, someone else would have noticed too."

"They would probably run off rather than admit to that," Cole comments.

Run off?

"Tomorrow, or I guess *today*, we should all go to classes like normal." Bree jots down a few more things and starts twirling a strand of her strawberry blonde locks.

"Except it won't be normal," Cole mutters.

"I will snoop around the kitchens and see what I can find," Bree continues, ignoring Cole's comment. "Poppy, try not to look so…" She looks me up and down. My eyes are red and puffy, and I am pretty sure I have mascara smeared across my face from rubbing my eyes repeatedly.

"Guilty?" I guess. "Messy?"

"Yeah, all of that." She raises her eyebrows and closes her notebook. "Let's get some sleep, everyone."

"Easier said than done," Cole responds.

* * *

I pace back and forth outside my front door. The sun is shining brightly, a little too bright for a day like this. The day I might possibly be hauled off to jail for a crime I definitely didn't commit. I knew I wouldn't be able to sleep at all, especially since one of the last things Cole mentioned before he left the apartment would not stop racing through my mind when I closed my eyes.

There was a student who ran off last semester without any explanation, and his name is Tom Fox. Figuring out why he left, and if it had anything to do with a kitchen ghost, is a good place to start. This is why I jumped out of bed early this morning and got one of the upper level students to let me into the bakery long enough to grab Tom's poster. I remembered that there was a contact number on it. I look down at the piece of wrinkled paper containing the phone number of someone named Brooke. I don't know a Brooke, nor have I heard that name thrown around in the hallway.

I bite the nail of my index finger, wondering if this is a stupid idea. It's a better idea than most and it's one that won't get me into trouble. The worst that could happen is that this Brooke woman hangs up on me. I don't have much more time before class, so I anxiously dial the phone number on my cell phone. It starts to ring, and immediately my chest begins thumping like a hearty loaf of sourdough being tossed on a counter.

"Hello?" It's the voice of a woman, and she sounds as if she's just waking up. She clears her throat. "Hello, who is this?"

"Hi," I answer. "I'm calling for someone named Brooke."

"I'm Brooke." She pauses and waits for me to state my business.

"Oh, hi," I say again.

"Hi," she answers a second time. "Can I help you?"

"Yes, I'm calling because I saw your name on a poster at my school. It was for a missing student? Tom Fox?"

The line becomes eerily silent. I hear a few voices in the background and the sound of a bell chiming before I hear the distinct sound of a door slamming shut. "Hello?"

"You know Tom?" she whispers. She breathes heavily as I shake my head, disappointed that I don't have some actual information for her.

"No, but I was wondering if I could ask you a few questions about him."

"I need to take that damn poster down," she replies. "I get prank calls, misdials, and booty calls up the yin-yang."

"Please," I blurt out before she hangs up. "I'm…writing a story about it." The lie slipped from my tongue out of desperation. "About the pressures of CPA…Calle Pastry Academy."

"It's about time someone did." She speaks a little louder. I hear the sound of a car pass by as if she is standing on a street corner. "But you've been misinformed. I can't help you."

"Oh," I respond. "You didn't know him that well?"

"I'm his girlfriend," she says proudly. "We met last semester when he came into the diner for drinks with some of his friends from the academy."

"So you of all people know how much pressure he was under to do well." I urge her in the right direction, hoping she'll spill something about how Tom saw something he shouldn't have or how he was accused of truffle thievery or something that I can relate to.

"Yes," she agrees. "He was usually pretty busy, but he wasn't stressed all the time. He told me he was one of the top students in his class. I believed him too. He made a killer grilled cheese with tomato."

"Then what happened last semester?" I ask.

Brooke takes a deep breath.

"The week before he disappeared he seemed tense about something," she admits. "I asked him about it once, but he kind of blew up in my face about it so I dropped it."

"I'm sorry."

"When I hadn't heard from him for a few days, I went to his apartment. He wasn't there."

"His roommate must have had some idea where he went," I add.

"He didn't have a roommate." I hear her sniffle. "I called him hundreds of times, but his number had been disconnected. I even tried calling his parents in Chicago. That number was disconnected too. No phone. Deleted social media accounts. It was like he vanished into thin air."

"Did you call the police?"

"They were no help," she sighs. "They said they couldn't do anything except make a few calls, since there was no evidence of foul play."

"So there was an investigation," I continue. I lean against the wall of my apartment building and pray that Brooke will give me something I can work with. My stomach churns as I wait for her reply.

"Yes. They questioned a few people, but that was about it. He was last seen leaving the student bakery still wearing his floury apron." Another sniffle. "Look, I don't want to talk about this anymore."

"I understand," I respond. "Sorry for bringing it up."

"I keep trying to move on, but—" She begins sobbing on the other end, and I stare down at my bare feet feeling guilty.

"I'm sure it had nothing to do with you." I try to sympathize with her, but I'm a wreck myself when it comes to relationships. I always feel like a hypocrite when I offer advice.

"Yeah, well." Another sniffle and a light cough. "I know you're only calling as part of your research, but a little tip?"

"Of course."

"Don't call someone you've never met before 9 a.m."

The moment she finishes her sentence, the line goes dead. I look at my cell phone, and walk slowly back into the apartment to get ready for my first class. Brooke must hate me for asking her for the dirty details of her boyfriend's disappearance. Good thing she doesn't know me.

CHAPTER TEN

Bree and I look straight ahead as we sit in Professor Sellers' class. We both noticed a few cops strolling around the grounds on our walk this morning, and one of the student kitchens is completely closed with a sign on the door referring students to another kitchen across campus. I can hear my chest pounding. Our classroom door opens, and part of me prepares to see his ghost waltz up front to tell me what a disgrace I am. I feel Bree squeeze my arm.

Miss Chester walks to the front of class and starts by opening her book. She glances at each student and quickly takes attendance. She doesn't look like she's been up all night crying, but she doesn't have the usual smile on her face. Of course, Georgina raises her hand.

"Where is Professor Sellers?" she asks.

"Unfortunately, Professor Sellers won't be teaching this class anymore." She glances down at the floor. "I am sorry to say this, but Stuart is no longer with us."

"What do you mean?" Georgina insists. I roll my eyes. "Is he sick?"

"I don't know much at the moment, Georgina." Miss Chester avoids making eye contact with her. "I will let you know when I hear more, okay?"

"He better not have quit," I hear Georgina mutter. "He said he was going to get me a list of the people judging the dessert contest."

"Okay," Miss Chester announces. "We're moving on to breads. Honey wheat people. Let's get going."

Bree heads to the storage room to grab our ingredients.

"Business as usual," I sigh.

"Poppy." The voice blasts through my ear and makes me jump.

"Jeff," I respond. "Hey."

"Hey," he replies, leaning against my station. "So, have you decided what you're entering in the contest yet?"

I swallow the lump in my throat and unclench my fists. I am expecting him to start asking questions about Professor Sellers, but I suppose I am just being paranoid. I sit up straighter on my stool and try to relax my shoulders. I have been feeling extremely tense all morning. Every door creaking and every person shouting makes me stop dead in my tracks. I expect the cops to burst through the doors any second to arrest me. I keep reminding myself to act normal.

Business as usual. Business as usual.

"No," I answer. At this point I am just hoping to survive the holidays.

"Do you need any help deciding?" He grins and casually runs his fingers through his blond hair.

"I would if I knew what to choose from," I respond.

"I hear you." He chuckles. "It needs to be something simple yet still professional. I've been thinking about making my famous biscotti." He leans in a little closer. "Don't go stealing my idea now."

"Oh, trust me," I respond. I force out a fake giggle to humor him. "That's the last thing on my mind."

"Yeah." He chuckles. "So, uh, what do say you come over tonight and give it a try?"

"You, me, and a biscotti?"

"Is it a date?" he asks.

I want to say *no*. I mean, I could barely swallow a mouthful of coffee this morning, and that is saying something. I don't think I can stomach Jeff and his charm too. My mind wouldn't even be in the room with us. I would much rather sit in my apartment while Bree bakes apple tartlets and reassures me that I am not going to jail.

"Is what a date?" Bree asks, returning from the pantry. She sets our ingredients on the table and begins getting ready to make sourdough bread.

"I am trying to convince Poppy here to come over to my place tonight," Jeff responds slyly.

"Oh really." Bree glares at me and nods. I shrug.

"What?" I say through my teeth.

"That sounds like a fabulous idea," Bree insists.

"It *does*?" I look at her like she's crazy, but Bree refuses to make eye contact.

"Yes," Bree insists. "She will be there."

"Great," Jeff says, looking at me as if I am the one who answered his question. "Whenever you're ready, you know where my place is."

"Yep." I bite the inside of my cheek and wait until Jeff is out of ear shot. I turn and slap Bree's arm.

"Owww," she mutters.

"*She'll be there*," I say, mimicking her. "What was that about?"

"Business as usual, remember?" Bree hands me a large bowl so I can get started on my dough.

"That doesn't mean I have to go on a date with Jeff."

"What is the matter with Jeff?" Bree whispers. "He's a good-looking guy."

"Then why don't *you* date him?"

Bree blushes.

"No," she answers quietly. "He's not my type. I don't date chefs."

"Silly me," I say sarcastically. "Of course you don't."

I carefully rub my eyes, trying not to smudge my eyeliner. I put on extra this morning to try and hide the bags under my eyes. It didn't work. I still look like a zombie every time I catch a glimpse of my reflection in my metal mixing bowl. I have cut back on all my black clothing since I have been here. Mostly because of how hot it is. But I love my mascara and eyeliner. I won't give up my smoky eyes.

I focus on my assignment. Thinking back to day one of classes, I can't believe I have gotten this far. I already feel like I know everything there is to know about pastries. After breads we will be doing a short section on confections. I am looking forward to setting the yeast aside for a while. Bree keeps reminding me that CPA offers a special wedding cake course for senior students who have already moved on to their internships and student bakery shifts. She wants me to take the class with her.

Cole on the other hand is crazy about the logistics of running a business. He is more concerned with the cost of goods sold than the actual taste of the goods, but he's still an excellent baker. He has been baking pies since he was twelve and had no problem making the school's famous southern peach pie on day one.

I am disappointed that we won't be spending a whole lot of time on the one dessert I am kind of obsessed with. Cupcakes. Maybe that is what I should make for the contest? That is, if I am not incarcerated by then.

I keep my mind on cupcakes as I finish making my bread dough. I remember walking past a cupcakery to and from rehearsals in NYC. The smell that wafted through the doors of that place was entrancing. If you closed your eyes it made you think you were at the top of a castle made of diamonds, surveying your cake-laden gardens. Every time I passed that cupcakery I told myself I would go in and buy one *tomorrow*, but I never did. I wasted all my chances, and now I might never know just how scrumptious those tiny morsels taste.

"Hey," Bree nudges me. "Cheer up."

"Huh?"

"You look like you are in a trance," she whispers. "You did nothing wrong, Poppy. You have nothing to hide. We will figure all this out."

I nod.

"I'm glad we ended up being roomies, Bree."

"Me, too."

"I am trying to stay positive, but..." Like Cole said, it's easier said than done.

"If it helps," she responds. "*Bree* isn't actually my name. I started calling myself that in middle school."

"Is it short for Breanna or something?"

"Beatrice," she mutters.

"Ewww," I tease. I smile for real. "Thanks, I *do* feel a little better now."

* * *

Jeff's dorm smells like he took an aerosol can of Old Spice and sprayed it on everything.

I mean *everything*.

The couch.

The carpet.

The drapes.

The kitchen towels.

His face.

I can't stop wrinkling my nose.

"Try this," Jeff says, handing me a cookie.

"This is a sugar cookie. What happed to your famous biscotti?" I am impressed to see that it's in the shape of a perfect circle, and the blue royal icing on top looks like a frozen pond. I lightly touch it. It dried perfectly.

"Yeah well, I'm trying out a few recipes before I make up my mind," he replies.

"Okay." I take a bite of the cookie, wishing I could smell it too. The top has a crunch to it and the inside of the cookie is soft. It tastes sweet and doughy with a lemony kick. "Do I detect a bit of lemon?"

"Is it too much?" he asks.

"No." I nod and take another bite. Jeff looks pleased with himself. He takes a seat next to me at the kitchen table. This date might have gone pretty well, if we were sitting outside away from the overpowering smell of cologne. I keep chewing to keep myself from wrinkling my nose.

"Oh," Jeff says, noticing how uncomfortable I am. "Sorry about the smell. It's my roommate."

"Thank heavens," I blurt out.

"I know," he comments. "It's a little much."

"Just a little." I plug my nose. Jeff laughs like I'm joking, but it's a relief to smell nothing for a few seconds. "Um, why don't we—"

"Take a walk?" he finishes. "I agree."

"Yeah." I stand up, taking my unfinished sugar cookie with me.

The two of us step into the humid afternoon. The sky is cloudy, but the heat still soaks into my bones. I am used to feeling sweaty all the time. I toss my dark hair over my shoulder and take another bite of the cookie.

"So do you miss being back home?" Jeff asks.

"Sometimes," I admit. "I miss being able to breathe."

He chuckles.

"Ballet, huh?" he continues. I catch him eyeing the length of my legs.

"It was my whole life until recently." I eye an open bench near the quad. I don't want to go walking past the student kitchens if I don't have to. I am sure the halls are filled with police officers by now.

"Sorry about that."

"It's okay," I reply. "Performing at a professional level for so long was grueling. I'm amazed that my body lasted as long as it did."

"I bet you were good."

"Compared to everyone else?" I respond. "I was average. Not terrible, but nothing show-stopping."

"Becoming a pastry chef is quite a career change," he comments. I glance at the color of his baby blue shirt. It matches his eyes. I wonder if he did that on purpose. My eyes dart to a tiny piece of royal frosting that dried on his sleeve.

"I grew up baking with my grandma." I pop the rest of my sugar cookie in my mouth, wishing I would have grabbed another one. "She came to school here and even opened up her own bakery."

"Then why didn't you jump right into pastry? Why spend all that time pursuing ballet?"

"That is an excellent question, Jeff." I sit on a bench next to a giant pot of purple flowers. I nudge his knee as he sits next to me. "I guess I felt like it was expected of me. My brother is an overachiever, and I guess I didn't want my parents to think that I wasn't as talented as him. They paid for me to go to a special school. When I turned eighteen I think I already knew that ballet wouldn't make me happy forever, but I didn't want to let them down. It's stupid, I know."

"No," he responds. "We all have moments like that." He sighs and glances up at the bright sky. "My parents almost had a meltdown when I told them I wanted to invent the world's first ever dessert bagel and sell them by the thousands. A toasted bagel with ice cream and sprinkles on top. You know, like the *new* banana split?"

"An up-and-coming fad," I chuckle. "Yes, that is a ridiculous dream."

"Sorry, I'm just kidding around. But it does sound rather original, doesn't it? Like *dessert contest* worthy?"

"Try it out," I encourage him, imaging the grotesque look on the judges' faces when they slice into a plain bagel with a scoop of vanilla ice cream in the center.

"Now you're trying to sabotage me." Jeff discreetly lifts his arms and places it on the back of the bench behind me. A patch of his skin brushes across my shoulder.

I feel my cell phone ringing. I hold up a finger and quickly answer it when I see Bree's name. My heart pounds as I say hello and wait to hear what she has to say. I keep a smile on my face so Jeff doesn't suspect anything.

"I figured something out," Bree says. "I asked Cole to come over."

"I hear you loud and clear." I don't even wait for her to say bye before I hang up. "Jeff, I'm sorry, but I've got to go."

"Oh."

"Girl stuff," I improvise. Jeff nods as if he would rather I not elaborate.

"You better go," he says. "I need to get to bed early anyway. My first shift at the student bakery is early tomorrow morning. Well, it's more of a *half* shift. Half of it is in the morning and half of it is in the evening."

"I thought our rotations don't start until next year?"

"I was picked to start them early," he responds. "Sweet, huh?"

"I guess." I stand up and take a deep breath. "Well, good luck tomorrow."

I begin walking back to my apartment when I hear Jeff shout something else. I turn around and see Jeff leaning back in his seat with a grin on his face. "Remember," he shouts, "we are even now."

CHAPTER ELEVEN

———

I don't have the heart to tell Bree that she isn't the only one who was picked by Mr. Harris to start working at the student bakery early. I walk through the door and find her beaming as she serves Cole a plate of warm doughnut holes. He grins as he takes a handful.

"Is she always like this?" he asks me.

"Nervous baker," I respond. Bree hears me from the kitchen and shrugs at my comment. "Okay spill, sister." I take a seat next to Cole and watch him inhale the doughnuts. He chews a little slower when he sees me staring.

"Okay." Bree takes a breath and opens her notebook. "I was able to take a look at the student kitchen where you found the professor. I had to duck under the yellow tape, but I did it."

"Look at you." I place a hand on her knee as if offering my congratulations. "You are the best roomie *ever*."

"Wait a minute," Cole interjects. "Are you positive that nobody saw you?"

"You would be surprised what a couple cops would do for a slice of apple pie." She lifts her chin looking pleased with herself.

"So what did you find?" Cole asks.

"You guys said there was a mess of flour everywhere, right?"

The two of us nod.

"Yeah," I answer. "It was everywhere."

"It wasn't flour."

"It wasn't?" Cole says.

"No, it was confectioner's sugar."

"Really?" I try to think of that piece of information as a clue that might give away who the murderer is, but I can't come up with anything.

"Yes," Bree reassures me.

"Just a minute." I stand up and retrieve my laptop from my bedroom. I am starting to feel less anxious and more eager to clear my name. I don't want to feel like I am getting nowhere. I return to the living room and open my computer. I search Shurbin Farms on the internet and pull up their website.

"What are you doing?" Bree asks.

"I think I need to crank this up a notch." I turn my laptop and show her the web page. It is yellow with pictures of peaches and the farm's logo near the top. A slideshow on the side of the website shows pictures of the fields and the historic house on the property, where the owners reside. A picture of their family flashes as I scan the rest of the introduction page for more information.

"Shurbin Farms," Cole says.

"I think we should go there."

"I don't know, Poppy."

"I know it's a clue. It *has* to be. Why else would Professor Sellers carry around a piece of paper with the words *Shurbin Farms* written on it?"

"A reminder that he's out of peaches?" Cole suggests.

Bree leans forward and studies the website.

"Come on." I narrow my eyes and glare at him. "We can go this weekend."

"Poppy," he mutters. "It's probably a waste of time."

"No, she's right," Bree says. "You two should go soon. I have to work the student bakery this weekend."

"Only if Poppy agrees to drive," Cole responds.

"Look." Bree clicks on a photo of the owner and his family. "Does he look familiar to you?"

I study the man in the photo, but his face doesn't ring a bell. I don't recognize him.

"Sorry," I answer. Cole studies the picture and shakes his head.

"From chapter one on our first day? The history of the school?" She shakes her head and points to the computer screen. "The owner looks just like Thomas Calle, the founder's son."

My skin gets goose bumps. Bree grabs one of her books and opens it to a photo of Francois Calle, the founder of the school, standing next to his son. My chest starts pounding when I realize that she's right. I hold the book next to my laptop and cover my mouth.

"I don't get it," Cole comments. "How is that even possible?"

"*We* are going to find out," I reply. "Have you ever been to Alabama?"

"Nope." He looks down at the floor. "But I'm sure it's better than jail."

* * *

There is a line of students waiting in the hall when Bree and I get to our afternoon class. Cole and I are leaving early tomorrow morning for Shurbin Farms in Alabama. I woke up this morning thinking it would be a mellow day. The police have been off and on campus, but they haven't really made their presence known until now.

"What's going on?" I see Cole anxiously clinging to his backpack.

"The cops are questioning us all," he says quietly. "All students from all classes."

My eyes go wide.

"Seriously? *Every* student?" I respond.

"The news just broke. Everyone all over campus is talking about it. They've finally come out and said that Professor Sellers is…you know."

"Crap," Bree mutters.

"Do you think they know about the ambulance and—"

"Duh," Cole cuts in. "*I* called them with *my* phone, and then you fainted. They know we were there that night."

I take a step back towards the front door.

"No, Poppy." Bree grabs my arm. "If you run, you'll look suspicious."

"I wasn't going to run," I argue. I take a step back again and this time Bree watches me. I walk back to the end of the line. Cole stares at me like I am a genius and follows.

I pick at my nails and anxiously lean against the wall thinking of nothing else than that night. I don't know what I should say to the police. Which parts will help me and which parts will hurt me? Another group of students walks through the doors. I casually step out of line and move to the back of the line a second time.

I tap my foot as I watch time dwindle away. Some of the students are complaining about waiting. Some of them are sitting on the floor studying. Others are whispering and looking around. I keep my mouth shut and continue to casually step out of line as soon as more students congregate behind us. Eventually we are the last ones, and there aren't many people ahead of us.

The door to the classroom opens, and Georgina steps out with tears in her eyes. She wails and looks up at the ceiling. It doesn't surprise me that she's making a scene. I try not to give her the attentions she wants.

"I can't believe this!" she cries. "I just can't believe it! Why? Why him?" She wipes perfectly formed tears from her cheeks.

"Drama queen," I murmur.

"What am I supposed to do now?" Georgina says as she passes us and heads for the exit. "I need that list of judges. Do you think he left it in his office?"

"And of course all she *really* cares about is the contest," Cole comments.

We take another step forward. Bree nudges my shoulder and shows me her watch. My heart leaps. It is time for our daily lecture from Mr. Harris. We might be free for the weekend. I am next in line to be questioned but before I can give one of the officers my name, Professor Sellers' next class arrives. The officer at the door glances at the time. I test my luck by slowly stepping away to walk to another classroom.

"Wait a minute," the officer barks. My chest tightens.

"We have another class to go to," I quietly reply.

"Give me your names first," he responds. I nod and give him my name. I breathe a sigh of relief when the three of us escape to our next class. I set my bag down on the counter and anxiously stare back at the door.

"Do you think they'll pull us out of class?" I whisper.

"Maybe." Bree shrugs. "At some point all of us will be questioned. It's just a matter of when."

Georgina bumps me as she walks past us to her seat. She glares at me and then laughs as she watches Cole sit at his station. She flicks a strand of her hair until it falls straight with the rest of her shiny ponytail.

"Nice going," she comments, looking at me. "He hated your work, so you had to go and bump him off. Very classy of you."

I feel my face going hot.

"What are you talking about?"

"Uh hello," she answers. "I'm talking about Professor Sellers dropping dead right before grades were due? Don't act all innocent."

"You think *I* had something to do with it?" I swallow the lump in my throat, and I'm starting to feel dizzy. Just when I thought I couldn't dislike Georgina any more than I already do, she goes and accuses me of murder.

"You *must* have." She smirks when she notices me shifting uncomfortably in my seat. "Like every question the police asked me was about you and Mr. Fedora over there." She glances at Cole.

"I wore that hat *once*," Cole responds, looking furious. Georgina giggles when she sees him shaking his head at her.

"What kind of questions did they ask?" I wait and hope she will answer honestly. Georgina keeps giggling as she looks at me and raises her eyebrows. She's enjoying this, and she is not going to tell me. *Shoot.*

"Don't listen to her," Bree whispers. "You did nothing wrong."

"I know but—"

"But," she continues, "the truth will come out. It always does."

CHAPTER TWELVE

———

I sit up at 4 a.m., wide awake because I couldn't sleep at all, not even with the Sleepytime Tea that Bree made me drink. The cricket living behind my dresser stops chirping as soon as I clear my throat. My thoughts are racing just as fast as they were when my head touched my pillow. I was lucky that I didn't have to talk to the police yesterday, but I feel like my luck is about to run out. All I can think about is finding the murderer, so I can get back to burning brownies and flattening soufflés. I hurriedly get dressed and throw a few clothes and toiletries into an overnight bag, just in case we stay in Alabama longer than we planned.

I walk quietly to the front door and take one last look at the living room before I step into the cool morning air. It is one of the few times of day I can breathe when I step outside. From what I hear, Alabama is just as humid and just as green.

My eyes dart to a freezer bag of double chocolate brownies on the coffee table. I smile when I see a note in Bree's handwriting wishing me good luck. I grab the bag and make the trek to Cole's apartment building. He will be happy when he sees what Bree made for us. I clutch the bag tight in my hand and scan the quad for cops. I see Cole walking towards me.

"Hey," I say, out of breath. I jog towards him.

"You couldn't sleep either?" he asks.

"Not a wink."

"Let's do this," he mutters.

We head towards the parking lot and get into my car. It's an old Honda with paint chipping on the passenger's door. I've had it since I graduated from high school. With all the time I used to spend in NYC, I left it at home in my parent's garage. There was no room for it at my studio apartment in the city, and I didn't really need it either. Mom insisted that I at least buy a new car before making my trip to Georgia, but I figured that one last adventure with it wouldn't hurt. After all, I've experienced a lot of *firsts* in this car. My first kiss. My first hangover. My first breakup.

"I hope you have AC, Lil' Mama."

"Yep," I say, starting the car. I slowly pull out of the parking lot and head towards the freeway entrance. I grip the wheel and feel my shoulders go tense when we pass the row of cop cars near the admin building. We pass them casually, and then I bolt towards the highway.

"You get anxious a lot," he comments. "Maybe you should lay off the espresso."

"Speaking of good stuff." I toss the bag of brownies at him. "From my roomie."

"Dang," he mutters as he opens the bag and basically swallows one of the brownies whole. "If that girl ever opens her own bakery I'm going to need a frequent buyer's card." He glances down at his abs which are, at the moment, tight and firm. "Or maybe a treadmill."

"I think cakes are more her thing. If she ever opens up her own business one day it will be a cake shop." I set my cruise control and head towards the Alabama state line. The freeway starts to look more and more rural. The sides of the road are covered with mossy green trees, and every few miles there are clearings in between the trees filled with murky water. I am still impressed with how similar the scenery is to back home in Oregon. If only the weather was similar too.

"What about you, Poppy? What are you going to do when you graduate?"

"Go back home for starters," I answer.

"You've never thought of staying in the South?"

"I don't know," I admit. "I guess I just assumed I would go back to Portland, because it's a familiar place. Or New York, since I spent the other half of my life there. I can't believe I used to go back and forth in between jobs just for…well, I won't make that mistake again." I prevent myself from bringing up my ex. The only reason I blew half my savings living between Portland and NYC was to see him when I could. I won't let a man con me like that ever again. Not if I can help it.

"Would you ever consider opening your own shop?" he suggests.

"Possibly." I smile at the thought of running things my way for once. Setting my own rules. Being my own boss. "I'm in love with cupcakes, you know. But there are a ton of cupcake shops back home already."

"So," Cole responds. "That shouldn't stop you."

"So are *you* going to open up a bakery?"

"Me?" Cole eats another brownie. "No. I'm going for a management position back in Atlanta. It's a guaranteed job for me once I graduate. Besides, if I open my own anything I want it to be a barbeque place."

"Tasty."

We continue talking until our conversation somehow turns to family. Cole tells me all about his older brothers, and I fill him in on the many pressures of growing up with a robot for an older brother. Mark is the kind of sibling that is absolutely perfect at everything. The kind of sibling that makes my parents sing his praises. Our discussion then turns to past relationships. I hold back as much as I can, but Cole has a way of prying information out of me. I don't mind. I feel like I can trust him with my thoughts. And I haven't had much of a chance to talk to anyone about my ex yet. Our breakup still feels fresh for some reason.

"So, what's his name?" Cole asks. "You do realize that every time you're about to say his name you stop yourself, right?"

"What does it matter what his name is?" I keep my hands firmly on the steering wheel. "He's an ex."

"Because saying someone's name out loud without cringing is the first step to getting over them." He folds his arms and stares at an upcoming road sign.

"Are you speaking from experience?"

"Maybe." He sighs and keeps his hands busy by playing with the collar of his shirt.

"Okay then, what's *her* name? Or can you not say it out loud yet either?"

"Emma," he states without cringing. "Emma, a year ago."

"And what happened? Did she cheat on you too?"

"No." He looks down for a moment and frowns. "We were engaged actually. And then one day she called the whole thing off. She said her and I just didn't click anymore. I guess we'd been growing apart for years, and we didn't even realize it."

"Until she met someone else," I comment.

He looks at me and rolls his eyes.

"Yes," he admits. "But she didn't cheat. She had the decency to tell me how she felt first."

"Well, I wish that were the case for me." I follow the next road sign with my eyes, but it passes by me so fast that I don't have time to read it. It's more of a distraction than anything. A distraction from remembering what I left behind on the West Coast.

* * *

"Oh," Cole blurts out. "Right here is our exit."

"Don't tell me it has already been a couple hours?"

Cole shrugs as I turn onto a county road leading to Shurbin Farms. We pass a sign saying we are a mile away from the main entrance. My stomach grumbles. Brownies aren't going to cut it. I need breakfast food. I feel relieved when I see a diner up ahead next to a tiny, ancient-looking gas station. I quickly pull up to the open sign and park the car. The small building looks as if it used to be a popular place, but the front windowsills are covered in dust, and the yellow paint surrounding the front entrance is fading. A sign on the door says *Peachtree Diner*.

"I knew you would stop for breakfast," Cole says. He hops out of the car. "Something to go?"

"Sure," I agree.

We walk into the diner. Most of the booths are empty, but a few tables are full of farmers sipping coffee. The walls are beige. The kind of beige that looks like it used to be white. The booths are red, and the floors are a white tile that feels a little sticky. A waitress looks up at us and beams.

"Take any seat you like," she shouts with a thick southern accent. The way she talks makes me forget all about the hint of southern twang in Cole's voice.

Every eye in the place is on us as we sit down. One thing about small towns like this is that out-of-towners are always gawked at. I grab a napkin and wipe the table even though it looks mostly clean. I grab a menu, but there is not much on it.

Eggs.

Bacon.

Pancakes.

Waffles.

Cheese grits.

Biscuits and gravy.

"Why do I get the feeling that not many travelers come here?" Cole whispers.

"Hi, I'm Bonnie Jean." The waitress places silverware on our table along with two cups of water. She has a pink clip in her light blonde hair and her fair skin is freckled. "Oh, I just love it when we get travelin' folk. It gives me the chance to practice my waitressin' skills. What can I get y'all?"

"Ummm." I stare down at my menu for a minute.

"Whatever you want, sweet pea, the cook will make it for you."

"Oh." I look at Cole. So much for a quick pit stop. "Can I have a few chocolate chip pancakes, some biscuits and gravy, and a side of bacon?"

"You got it," Bonnie Jean replies. "I love it when little ladies like yourselves have big appetites." She looks to Cole. "What about you, hun?"

"Do you still have any country fried chicken?"

"Of course."

"I'll have that," Cole responds.

"With a buttermilk waffle?" she asks. Cole nods. Bonnie Jean leaves our table and races into the kitchen. I hear her yell our orders to the cook like she's scolding her husband for leaving the toilet seat up.

"I guess we'll be here for a while," Cole says.

"That'll give us some time to figure out how we are going to do this," I respond. "We can't just walk up to the owner's house, ring the doorbell, and ask him if he's ever heard of a man named Thomas Calle."

"Why not?"

"Because we'll probably get kicked out if we did that," I answer. "That's why not."

"You're forgetting that people here are friendlier than you're used to. Not like New Yorkers or folks on the West Coast who rush everywhere even when they don't have to." He takes a sip of his water. "No coffee?"

"You told me to lay off, remember?"

"Oh right," he comments. "Anyway, we'll ask around and fish for an introduction. Then we can bring up CPA and see how he reacts."

"What if he doesn't?" I ask. I place my elbows on the table and glance out the window at the sun glowing over a cluster of willow trees. "What if this whole thing is a dead end?"

"It's not." Cole glances back at the kitchen as Bonnie Jean dashes out with a tray of food. "If it makes you feel any better I will mention Professor Sellers if things aren't looking good. It might be a bad idea, but I'll do it."

"Okay," I say. I watch our waitress set a plate of chocolate chip pancakes in front of me. She hands me a few packets of butter and maple syrup. The smell of fried chicken makes my stomach rumble. Cole's eyes go wide when he stares at his plate. "I wasn't expecting the food to look so—"

"Delicious?" Cole finishes my sentence.

* * *

Shurbin Farms looks like the pictures on the website. The entrance is a mile long road with trees planted on both sides. In between the tree are fields. We pass a section that looks like a dead vineyard. All the grapes have been picked, and the vines are thin, dark sticks swirling around each other. The look of it all shriveled like that gives me chills.

I pull up to a little hut where other cars are parked. I watch as a family with two small children, a boy and girl, jump up and down, each with their own picking baskets. My family never had time to do things like this. Weekends were always full of homework, recitals, and competitions.

We came too late in the season for blackberry and blueberry picking. A sign in the parking says what is available for picking today – okra, collard greens, persimmons, apples, and figs. Another sign next to it says, "*Tangerines and clementines coming soon.*" Cole and I take a basket and grab a map of the farm.

"Ready?" Cole asks.

"I could use a good nap." I touch my stomach. It feels as full as it did the first time I visited the student bakery. "Why do I always binge eat when I'm around you?"

"Let's do this." He ignores my comment and focuses on finding the owner's residence. He holds open his map and points straight ahead of us. A cool breeze keeps me from overheating. It even feels a little too chilly.

I follow Cole through a field of tall grass until I see a house in the distance. It is a white plantation home with shutters and flower boxes framing each window. Two white columns support a second patio that runs the length of the second floor.

Cole and I walk as fast as we can. My heart pounds. I wipe away the sweat on my forehead. I match Cole's speed until we are standing at the front door. I wait a second before I knock. This is either the worst or the best idea I have ever had.

"Just do it," Cole mutters.

I gently ring the doorbell.

I hear barking inside the house. The door opens, and a young girl in short jean shorts and a tank top answers the door. She has an earbud in one of her ears, and her hair is in a ponytail. She slips an iPod into her pocket and clears her throat.

"Can I help you?" she asks. "We stopped doing tours back in August." I put my picking basket behind my back.

"No, I'm actually here to speak with the owner."

"Oh my dad," she responds. "Uh, who should I say is here?"

I glance at Cole.

"Friends," Cole lies.

"Right." The girl chuckles. "Wait just a minute." She shuts the door.

"Friends? Really?" I put a hand on my hips. I grab his picking basket and set it down on the porch next to mine. "Now he's going to think we're tourist creeps or something."

"Do you think he would come to the door if we said we were nosey students here to ask questions?" Cole answers.

"Good point."

The door opens again. This time a man answers it. His hair is turning gray, and his nose is pointy like the pictures I have seen of Francois Calle. He's wearing jeans and a collared shirt that brings out his hazel eyes. I try not to scare him by leaping for joy. I automatically reach for Cole's hand and squeeze it. He glances at me, and my heart beats a little faster when our eyes lock together.

"Yes," the man says. "Do I know you?"

"Sorry to bother you sir, but we were wondering if we could ask you a few questions?" Cole waits for him to agree.

"Look," the man replies. "I am very busy today and—"

"Please," I add. "It's really important." The man sighs and takes a step back like he's about to close the door. "At least tell us if you knew a man named Thomas Calle?"

The man stops and stares at me.

"Where did you hear that name?" he asks.

"We are students at Calle Pastry Academy."

"Oh." He sighs. "You two better come inside."

I look at Cole. He nods at me and gently places his hand on my back. He follows me inside where a faint sparkle makes my eyes dart up at the ceiling. A chandelier with crystals that reflect sunlight everywhere is hanging above a circular table with a decorative bowl of apples in the middle of the foyer.

"I'm James," the man says as he reaches out to shake my hand.

"Poppy Peters."

"Cole." Cole glances suspiciously up the staircase.

"What's that smell?" I ask. I sniff the air and find myself thinking back to last year's Thanksgiving feast. I bite the side of my lip.

"My family meets every weekend for a special lunch," James says. "Come through here." He leads us past a giant kitchen with antique, white cabinets and a wall of grayish stones above the stovetop. It looks like a kitchen straight out of *Country Living Magazine*.

We end up in a large study. The walls are lined with bookshelves, and there is wooden desk in the corner. James sits on a leather couch with his hands on his knees. Cole and I sit across from him, and I notice that Cole is staring at the silver watch on James's wrist.

"We won't take up too much of your time," I say.

"It's okay." James smiles. "I'm surprised that no one from your school has contacted me sooner."

"Why is that?" Cole asks.

"Well, son." James leans forward. "That man you mentioned, Thomas Calle? He just happens to be my father."

"But the legend of Old Man Thomas..." I don't know what else to say to make sense of the things I heard in the kitchen on my first day at the academy. I had been telling myself it really was a ghost all this time, but it turns out that Old Man Thomas might have not mysteriously died at all. "I thought he died or disappeared or something?"

"Oh, he did," James answers. "He ran away and ended up here. Mr. Shurbin took him in, and Dad worked on the farm until Mr. Shurbin died. He had no other living relatives, so he left this place and all of its staff to him."

"Whoa," Cole gasps. "Then technically the school belongs to you."

"No." James shakes his head. "After Dad ran away, his father took him out of his will. The school doesn't belong to my family anymore."

"But I'm sure you could get a lawyer and—"

"No," James continues. "Dad didn't say much about that place until he was well-ridden with old age, but I know that he never wanted to go back."

"Why did he leave?" I ask.

"He opened up about it right before he passed. He actually seemed relieved to be talking about the school so openly again. He had *tons* of stories." James folds his arms and looks at the bookshelf in front of him as he talks. It is like he's watching his memories play out in front of him. "He had an argument with one of the teachers. The teacher had told him what a disappointment he turned out to be, and that's when Dad decided that the school would be better off without him."

"Which teacher?" Cole asks.

"Oh, he's probably not around anymore," James replies. "I don't even think I remember the name." He looks up at the ceiling for a moment with a grin on his face as if reminiscing about his dad. "I guess most of the founding teachers wouldn't be around anymore. Though last I heard there are still two fellows there who might have known Dad."

"Mr. Dixon?" Cole says. James shakes his head. "He's the president of the school now."

"Yes," James replies. "And that other old gentleman."

"Mr. Harris?" Cole asks. "He's the oldest teacher still there, I think."

"Yep, that must be them."

"Wow," I comment. "All these years and no one knew that Buzz, I mean Thomas Calle, was only a state away."

"It's funny how things work out sometimes." James nods and stands up.

"One more thing," I add. "Do you know any of the newer teachers? Say a man named Stuart Sellers?" I can feel Cole staring at me, hoping that James admits that he does.

"Stuart Sellers?" James asks. I lean forward until I'm on the edge of my seat. "As a matter-of-fact he called me up not too long ago."

"Seriously?" I gulp.

"Yeah," James says sincerely. "He wanted to know a few things about our latest shipment of peaches." He clears his throat. "Why don't you two stay for lunch? You have a long drive ahead of you."

"Oh, um," I stammer. "I don't want to impose."

"Don't be silly," James responds. "Come on. I was just about to make something I *know* you'll enjoy." He smiles and heads back towards the kitchen. I look at Cole and raise my eyebrows.

"We shouldn't have eaten so much for breakfast," I mutter.

CHAPTER THIRTEEN

———

James pulls ingredients from the cupboards and grabs a handful of peaches from a fruit bowl on the kitchen table. He begins peeling the peaches, and right away I know what he's making. He is making Francois's famous peach pie. I watch him curiously as he cuts chunks of butter for the dough.

"You can probably make this in your sleep," James comments. I look to Cole. He is staring at the oven which is emitting the delightful smell of roast turkey.

"Not exactly," I say quietly. "I kind of bombed my first day."

"Well here." James passes me the bowl. "Let's see you at work."

I nervously nod and begin adding more ingredients to the dough. I begin mixing it with my hands like I did the first day of class. Cole sits at the kitchen table and starts chatting with a petite woman who just entered the room with a basket full of produce.

"Whoa." James stops me. "Take your time. We're not in a hurry here." He urges me to knead the dough slower. "You know, I've had tons of peach pies in my day but nothing beats this one. Do you want to know why?" I shrug. "Because my Dad used to make it for me."

"I used to bake with my grandma," I respond. I smile thinking about those Sunday afternoons we spent together. "She used to make these amazing little candies that she learned how to make in South America where she grew up."

"And I bet if you made those now you would enjoy every step of the process," James responds.

"Yeah." I watch him mix the peach filling as I think about Grandma Liz and the way she used to tease my dad for still cutting the crust off of his sandwiches.

"It's comfort food." James puts the pie together with little effort. His hands seem to move on their own, having memorized each step since infancy. "The food we eat that brings us back to those cherished moments. The turkey, collard greens, and peach pie will always remind me of family."

"I don't know if I've ever thought of food that way."

"Mary Ann, darling." James looks at the woman who is showing Cole her basket of persimmons. "This is Poppy and Cole. They're visiting from Georgia."

"Oh really?" Mary Ann replies. She's tan with blonde hair. She looks younger than James. "What brings you two to the farm?"

"They're from the academy," James adds.

"Oh." She has a surprised look on her face. "We've never had visitors from there before. Isn't this a treat?"

I smile and watch James proudly put the pie in one of his ovens. He has two that are stacked on top of each other. I help Mary Ann set the table, and Cole volunteers to make the collard greens. He immediately grabs a pot and gets to work on cooking them. James's daughter comes to the table and brings her teenage boyfriend who has on a beanie that covers most of his head. I try not to laugh when James gives him the stare down. Mary Ann's parents arrive promptly after that along with her brother and younger sister. When James's step-sister hollers at the door, I start to wonder if we are going to have enough food.

Mary Ann pulls the turkey out of the oven as well as a giant pan of roasted potatoes. I help Cole bring everything to the table, and James's family welcomes us like we're family. The aroma in the room is enough to make me forget about breakfast. I am excited to eat and create more food memories, as James would put it.

The last person to arrive at the table is an older man with a weathered face. He is wearing jeans paired with cowboy boots, and the sleeves of his shirt are rolled up revealing thick forearms that have probably tossed thousands of bales of hay. He nods at James and glances at Cole and I suspiciously as he sits down.

"This is my right hand man, Dirk. His dad worked with my dad." James introduces us to the man. "Dirk, this is Cole and Poppy. They are visiting from Georgia."

"Where abouts in Georgia?" Dirk asks. He has dark hair and dark eyes that fixate on me when he talks.

"Calle Pastry Academy," I reply. For a brief second, he looks like he's biting the inside of his cheek to prevent himself from blurting out an unwanted response.

"Ah yes," he finally remarks. "One of our many customers. I take it our peaches are still shining in those pies of yours."

"Yes sir," Cole answers.

"Well, everyone," James says. He waits until the whole table is quiet. "Dig in."

My elbow bumps Cole as I reach for a roll.

"They used to make those rolls in the student bakery," James comments.

"No kidding." I have half the roll already stuffed in my mouth.

"Yeah." James takes a sip of his beer. "I guess they don't ever make them anymore."

"They still make the orange rolls," Cole comments.

"Yes, Dad's orange rolls." He chuckles. "I loved those when I was a kid. What about the blueberry scones?"

"Oh yeah," Cole responds. "And the beignets."

"Oh yes," James replies over his wife's chatter. "They've been making those since the school opened." He puts a forkful of turkey in his mouth. I copy him but add a bit of potato to mine. "As a matter-of-fact, one of the teachers was making a batch the night that Dad left. I remember him telling me that story like it was yesterday." He chuckles and takes another sip of beer. "Dad was so upset that the guy called him a no-good, lazy bastard that he knocked over a few mixing bowls. The place was covered in powdered sugar." He sighs and fills his mouth with collard greens.

"Powdered sugar," I mutter. "Confectioner's sugar." My eyes go wide as my mind jumps back to when Bree mentioned that the kitchen where we found the professor was actually covered in confectioner's sugar, not flour. "James." He looks up at me. "So you're saying that the night your dad ran away he had an argument in one of the kitchens?"

"Yes," James confirms.

"And he got so upset that he knocked a few things over and powdered sugar flew everywhere?" I continue to ask.

"Yes." James laughs. "What is it with you guys and beignets? That Stuart fellow asked me about them too."

"Are you sure you're remembering correctly, sir?" Dirk interjects. "I seem to remember your dad mentioning that he left because of an ex-girlfriend or something. Not a kitchen debacle." He glances at me like I'm a fly in his soup.

"It's been so long that all of Dad's stories seem to run together nowadays." James chuckles.

"You can't believe everything you hear, ain't that right." Dirk watches me with a bothered expression as I continue asking questions. He narrows his eyes and presses his lips together when I open my mouth to speak.

"Stuart Sellers, our teacher, asked you about our beignets?" My torso feels rock solid. I take a deep breath and try to calm myself down.

"Yeah, he wanted to know how long, in all my dealings with the school, the student bakery has been making them. 'Since the day it opened,' I told him."

Cole puts his fork down and glances at me. Professor Sellers was onto something. I don't know why black truffles, beignets, and powdered sugar fights led to his death, but my heart is pounding. I know we are closer to solving this mystery and clearing my name so I can remain a pastry student.

I anxiously wait for the end of our meal so Cole and I can speed back to Georgia and tell Bree what we found out. I take another bite of turkey, but this time I am so distracted that I don't even notice how moist and spicy it tastes. I mindlessly shove more potatoes into my mouth as Mary Ann talks about their recent harvest and a new recipe she found for persimmon pudding.

"I see you've been eyeing this, son," James says across the table. I can hardly hear him, because James's teenage daughter just turned the volume of her iPod on full blast. The entire table is forced to listen to pop music as they chew their food.

James looks down at his watch. He holds up his wrist, giving Cole a closer look at it. Cole grins as his eyes admire the craftsmanship. He nods and raises his eyebrows.

"One day I want to get me one of those," Cole comments.

"This watch was a gift from Dirk." James exhales and glares at his daughter until she turns down the volume of her music. "I don't think I'd ever buy a Rolex for myself, but the crops have been good this year."

"I'd say they've been *more* than good," Dirk adds, looking pleased with himself, but his smirk disappears when he rests his eyes on me. It's starting to make me feel uncomfortable.

I feel Cole's elbow bump me, and I look at him. He raises his eyebrows and takes a tiny bite of collard greens. He wants to get back to school just as much as I do. I can see his firm chest heaving. I bite the inside of my cheek to stop myself from overeating again. I look down at my plate, surprised to see that most of my food is gone.

James's daughter turns her music up a second time, having been coaxed by her boyfriend. She begins dancing comically at the table, moving her hips in her chair and letting her hair fall across her face. She ignores her mother's warning to turn her music off until dinner is over. James's face begins turning red as if he's about to burst. He bangs his hand on the table. "Jessica, how many times do I have to tell you?" His daughter jumps to her feet ready for an argument. She begins spouting off a dramatic monologue that she seems to have practiced a few times.

Cole chuckles and gently cups my elbow with his hand to pull my attention towards him.

"Someone was in the kitchen making beignets the night Professor Sellers died," Cole whispers. "Why?"

"Late night snack?" I suggest. Cole shakes his head. Jessica screams something about how her boyfriend isn't a tool, he is just *misunderstood*.

"That sort of explains the legend of Old Man Thomas." He chuckles to himself. "The banging of pots and pans in the middle of the night. Clearly, those old ghost stories came from the night he ran away."

"Yep." I look around the table and notice that Mary Ann is finished eating. She stands up and starts collecting empty plates, avoiding her daughter's mental breakdown like it is an everyday occurrence. It very well might be.

"I told you there was no ghost," Cole says proudly. "It was all a myth."

"That still doesn't explain the noises I heard the first day of school," I reply.

"I guess not." He thinks for a minute and puffs out his chest. "But it *wasn't* a ghost."

"Fine," I agree. "It wasn't the ghost of Old Man Thomas."

"Thank you," he mutters.

James stands up to grab another cold beer right as his daughter stamps her foot and drags her boyfriend upstairs to her room.

"Well," James announces, as if the entire argument never happened. "Who wants pie?"

* * *

Our drive back to CPA is quieter than I thought it would be. First of all, Cole and I are both so stuffed that we can hardly move in our seats. I watch tree after tree pass, thinking of nothing but beignets, peach pie, and murder. I have replayed James's story so many times in my head that I think I might go insane, and I keep trying to figure out why Dirk seemed so annoyed with me. Maybe that is just the way that he is?

"Did Dirk seem a little odd to you?" I throw the question out there hoping that Cole noticed it too.

"What do you mean?"

"I mean, did you see the way that he looked at me?" I go on. "It was like *I* was the one disrupting dinner instead of Jessica. What was up with that?"

"I didn't notice," he answers.

"Yeah, you were too busy fantasizing about Rolex's. I highly doubt a simple farm makes *that* kind of money."

"Don't judge, Poppy. We're not in the produce business. Maybe they really did have a good harvest this year?"

"True," I agree.

"Anyway." Cole chuckles. "I thought Jessica put on one hell of a show. And don't get me started on that dude she was with." He pauses and rubs his eyes, no doubt fighting off the inevitable nap that follows when you stuff your face with too much turkey. "On second thought, maybe you are right about Dirk. I thought he was going to try and yank my arm out of its socket when he shook my hand before we left."

"Okay," I sigh. "You're going to have to get me off this for a while, or I'm going to have a meltdown trying to figure this all out."

"Right." Cole turns towards me. "Let's hope that Bree doesn't have a strawberry cheesecake or a rhubarb pie waiting for us when we get home. I don't think I'll be able to say no."

"*Pig*." I laugh. He grins and folds his arms. I glance at his biceps and then quickly look away when my cheeks feel flushed.

"You know what we need to do?"

I can feel Cole staring, and it makes my heart start drumming. I grip the wheel a little tighter and focus on the road ahead.

"What?" I ask.

"Snoop." He scratches his chin. "Oh, sorry to bring this up again, but I think we need to get back in that kitchen and do some serious sleuthing."

"And what would we even be looking for? Bree already looked around and figured out that what we thought was flour was in fact powdered sugar." I giggle. "The two of us suck at sleuthing."

"Then we need to get better," he continues. "What better time than now?"

"Okay," I agree. "We'll go back. That is, if one of us isn't hauled away to jail before then."

CHAPTER FOURTEEN

———

Bree is pacing nervously around the living room when we walk through the door. She breathes a sigh of relief and urges us to sit down. We made it back before dinner, but I expect that Bree has already eaten another one of her frozen dinners after a long shift at the student bakery. I glance in the kitchen, thankful that she doesn't have another tasty dessert waiting for us. I can't swallow another morsel.

"I'm surprised you didn't make pecan sandies or something," I comment.

"I made oatmeal raisin cookies this morning, but I accidentally ate them all." Bree sighs.

"How do you *accidentally* eat something?" Cole asks.

Bree ignores him and grabs the water bottle sitting on the coffee table. She gulps it down before she looks at us again. My muscles go tense as I wait for her to speak.

"The police came this morning," Bree says. "They were looking for you." She stands up and peeks through the blinds. "They could be back any minute."

"What?" I gasp.

"It's your turn to be questioned," Bree continues. "When I told them you weren't here they were not happy." She hands me a card with a phone number on it. "A detective guy wants me to give you this. He wants you to call him as soon as you get home."

"Do you think they'll lock me up?" I gulp.

"Don't give them a reason to," Bree responds. She looks at Cole. "I think the two of you should just tell the truth."

"That we broke into the professor's office?" Cole responds. "No thanks."

"Whatever we tell them our stories need to match," I instruct.

"And they'll eventually find out that you guys were nosing around in the professor's office," Bree adds. "Maybe you should take your chances?"

"We might not need to," I say. "Cole and I met the son of Thomas Calle."

Bree's eyes go wide. She stands up and starts anxiously peeking through the blinds again.

"What did he say?"

"Cole and I think all the stories about the ghost of Old Man Thomas come from the night he ran away. He had an argument with someone in the kitchens. He was so angry that he threw a few things, but that's not the strangest part." I pause to let Bree process the information. "The night Thomas ran away, whoever he argued with was making *beignets*. Powdered sugar was thrown all over the place."

"Like the night the professor was murdered," she mutters.

"Exactly," Cole chimes in. "We've decided to go back to the student kitchen and see if we can find anything else."

"I don't think that's a good idea anymore." Bree shakes her head. "That detective guy has been stalking that building all day. You'll look even more suspicious."

"We have to *try*," I argue. "Tonight."

"We will need some kind of distraction," Cole says. "It will only give us a few minutes to sneak in, but it's worth it, right?"

"The detective knows the three of us are friends," Bree points out. "Do either of you know anyone else who might help?" She looks at me as she says it. I roll my eyes.

"I think I know someone," I reply. "If we hurry we might be able to catch him ending his shift."

"Shift?" Bree asks.

My chest tightens. I never told Bree about Jeff working at the student bakery.

"Yeah," I admit. "He sorta kinda was asked to work at the student bakery too."

"What?" she pouts. "I thought he was there washing dishes for extra credit?"

"You can do that?" I fold my arms. "Why didn't you tell me?"

"Who are you guys talking about?" Cole looks annoyed. His forehead is crinkled as he looks from me to Bree.

"Jeff," I blurt out. Cole immediately frowns.

"*That* dude won't help us," he answers.

"He will because he has a thing for Poppy," Bree insists.

My cheeks start to feel warm so I quickly change the subject.

"Let's go. Who's ready? *I am.*" I race out the door before Bree has more time to tell me all about the men who are looking for me. I am too close to clearing my name to quit now. I dash across the quad, practically running. I hear footsteps behind me as Cole and Bree struggle to catch up. I wipe my forehead when I reach the bakery doors. The blast of AC when I walk in reminds me of my first day in Georgia. I remember hardly being able to breathe as I waited in line for one of Buzz's rise and shine orange rolls. That day feels like it was years ago. I had no clue what I was in for back then.

I inhale the smell of gooey cinnamon rolls and look behind the counter. My eyes dart to the tray of beignets. Such a mischievous dessert those things are turning out to be. I glare at them as if they are intimidated by my death stare.

Why do they have to smell so good?

Jeff walks out of the kitchen looking surprised to see me. He grins as he collects the almost empty tray of raspberry Danishes. I put on my best smile and prepare to be flirtatious. I haven't thought through what I am going to say to him. I will have to wing it and hope he agrees to keep watch for me or distract a cop while I snoop around the crime scene. Too bad there's no time for Bree to bake a fresh apple pie.

"Poppy," Jeff says. He lightly touches his hair net. "I didn't think I would be seeing you here."

"Please tell me your shift is almost over," I respond.

"It ended a while ago, but I volunteered to stay a little longer. Raspberry Danish?" He holds up the tray and urges me to take one of the leftovers.

"No thanks," I say. "Wow, I didn't know you were such an overachiever."

"That's me." He grins wider. The bakery door chimes, and Jeff directs his attention behind me. "Let me help these customers, and we can hang out."

"Okay." I watch Jeff fill a box full of beignets for two men wearing T-shirts and jeans. Jeff grabs each one from the front of the tray and happily hands the men their box. They nod as he quickly rings them up on the register. When the men leave, Jeff takes off his hair net.

"Done." He smiles. "So what were you thinking? Practicing for the contest? Homework? Dinner?" I feel a little queasy when he mentions going out to eat. I have had enough food today to last me all month.

"A little field trip?" I suggest.

"I trust you will be staying *in* the country?" a voice says behind me. I turn around and see Bree shrugging. Cole has his head down, and a man in a tie is standing next to them with two cops in uniform. I gulp.

My time is up.

"What's going on?" Jeff asks.

"I was never pulled in for questioning yesterday," I respond, looking at the detective.

"Poppy, is it?" The detective shakes my hand. His short hair is chestnut brown. It matches the scruff on his chin. The man is taller and younger than I was expecting him to be. He would still tower over me even if I was wearing my high-heeled boots.

"Yes."

"I am Detective Reid. I am going to have to ask you to come with me."

"Okay." I nod. I can't avoid it any longer, and I'm not feeling stupid enough to run. I follow Detective Reid outside and across the quad to an empty classroom.

"You first," the Detective says to me. I enter the classroom with one of the policemen. The other one stays in the hall with Bree and Cole. My hands shake as I sit across from Detective Reid. He looks down at a folder when he speaks to me.

"I know what you're thinking," I say.

"And what is that?" he asks.

"I'm about to be expelled and I wasn't exactly the professor's favorite student. You have to believe me though. I did *not* kill him." My voice quivers slightly at first, but I eventually find my confidence.

"So you did find him that night?" he asks.

"Yes," I gulp.

"What were you doing in the kitchens so late?"

"Would you believe me if I said I was studying?" I shrug. It's worth a try.

"Look Poppy," Detective Reid says. He rubs his eyes like he hasn't slept in days. "I want to help you, but you have to help me. I realize that telling me the truth feels like the risky thing to do, but you need to weigh your options here. Becoming a murder suspect is serious stuff."

I slump my shoulders as I have an inner debate with myself. I have to tell him the truth. Maybe he can help me piece together this puzzle.

Or maybe he is an absolute dirtbag.

"Fine." I take a deep breath. I search for the right words. Words that don't make me sound like a shady truffle thief. "Have you already spoken to Mr. Dixon about me?"

"He gave me your file," he says honestly.

"So you know about the package of missing black truffles?"

"I do." The detective nods. I tap my fingers on the countertop as I think back to how that night began.

"I didn't steal them," I say quickly. "I was in the kitchen practicing for the school contest coming up. I made puff pastry dough for napoleons, which ended up being thrown away. Probably by one of my classmates who doesn't think much of me. Anyway, I decided to leave when I heard noises coming from the kitchen next door. When I got into the hallway I saw Professor Sellers."

"What kind of noises did you hear?" he asks.

"Pots. Pans. You know, kitchen noises."

"That was the night the black truffles were stolen?" he confirms.

"Yes." I nod. "The next day Mr. Dixon pulled me into his office and said I would be expelled if the thief wasn't caught. I guess Professor Sellers told him I was the only student in the building at that time. He thinks I am guilty."

"Then what happened?" Detective Reid is writing furiously.

"I decided to snoop around to try and clear my name." I look down at the floor and take a calming breath. I still don't know if I am doing the right thing by telling him all this. "I snuck into the professor's office after hours, because I thought maybe *he* was the one who stole the truffles, and that's when I heard a scream." I gulp. The memory is beginning to re-live itself in my head. "We ran to the kitchens, and that's when we saw him."

"We?"

I blush.

"Yeah," I respond. "Cole, that guy in the hallway, was with me. He was only trying to help."

"I see," he responds. "Well, I appreciate your honesty." He keeps a straight face as he writes. I can't help but roll my eyes. It was hard for me to dive into those memories again, and he won't even give me a reassuring nod.

"Sure you do." I watch him until he looks up. "Is this the part where you arrest me and say thanks anyways?"

"No." He allows himself to chuckle. "This is the part where I ask you to stay near campus, because I'll be contacting you *real* soon."

"To arrest me?"

"I could just arrest you now if you prefer?" he jokes.

"No thanks." I stand up to leave. "Are we done here?"

"One more thing," the Detective adds. "How many kitchens does the school have?"

I wrinkle my nose.

"I don't know," I respond. "Quite a few. There are three or four in this building and some across campus where the more advanced students meet."

"Are there kitchens anywhere else?" he asks.

"The dorms and apartment buildings? But those are more *kitchenettes,* if you ask me."

"Thank you," he says. He glances at the officer standing next to him. "Rope them all off." Detective Reid looks at me again. "You can go now, Miss."

I raise my eyebrows as I walk out the door. Cole and Bree look worried. They eagerly wait to see what I do when I exit the room. I stroll right up to Cole and put my hand on his shoulder.

"I told them everything," I whisper.

He shakes his head.

"Poppy, you can't trust the po-po. Have I taught you nothing?" I hear him grind his teeth as he slowly walks into the classroom for *his* interrogation.

"He'll get over it," I whisper to Bree. I take a deep breath and realize I lied to Detective Reid without realizing it. There is one more kitchen that I forgot to mention to him, and it is in the student bakery. Whoever has been sneaking around will have no choice but to use that kitchen unless they want to make that kind of noise in one of the dorms where there are paper-thin walls. "I have a plan, and it involves some extra strong tiramisu."

CHAPTER FIFTEEN

———

I was only joking about the tiramisu, but Bree made one anyway. After I mentioned it, she couldn't get it out of her head. All I wanted was coffee that I could eat by the spoonful, because my plan involved staying up late.

"Do you think we are under surveillance?" Bree whispers.

"Maybe?"

It's midnight, and I am dressed in a pair of black leggings and a black top. I taste the coffee as I take another bite of Bree's tiramisu. My heart is pounding. This might be one of the gutsiest things I've ever done, apart from confronting Mom one Christmas when she almost sold my car while I was away.

I just hope that I get lucky.

"If Cole doesn't show soon I'm leaving without him," Bree mutters.

"So you are positive that the student bakery is open tomorrow?"

"Yes," she says impatiently. "For the hundredth time, yes. I overheard princess Georgina saying she was asked to run the kitchen until closing time. Geez, Mr. Harris is handing out early rotations like candy."

"Waking up at 3 a.m. is not a *sweet* reward," I remind her.

"But it scores me brownie points." Bree pulls down the hem of her black party dress. It is the only black thing she has in her wardrobe.

"Are you sure you'll be able to run in that?"

"Who says we are running?" she asks. "What would we be running from? I thought we were going to snoop around the crime scene again?" She takes a deep breath and smiles. "Man, I love a good mystery."

That's because she's not the one being considered as a suspect.

"Let's just go," I say, opening the front door.

"What about Cole?"

"Maybe he forgot to set his alarm clock or something?" I respond. "We don't have time to wait. I really hope this works."

I quietly walk down the street and across the quad. No one is in sight. I glance at our usual student building. Bree begins moving towards it, but I keep walking. She jogs to catch up with me. I stop and hide in the shadow of a tree as Bree practically waddles in her dress to keep my pace. She leans over and catches her breath.

"What are you doing?" she whispers. "You are going the wrong way."

"No, I'm not." I look forward at the student bakery. Bree follows my gaze and widens her eyes.

"Poppy," she scolds me. "We are *not* breaking into the bakery."

"Relax," I reply. "If I am right, we won't have to break in."

I continue walking quietly. My eyes scan from left to right looking for cops or crooks who might be following us. My hand brushes the front doors, and I peer inside. The bakery is dark. I keep walking along the edge of the building as Bree keeps a hand on my shoulder. I hear her gulp.

"Poppy," she whispers. "I changed my mind. I say we wait for that hot detective to solve this one."

"You thought he was hot?" I ask. I sneak towards the back door leading to the kitchen.

"Didn't you?"

"If you set aside his dull personality," I respond. "Sure."

"Uh-huh." Bree quietly giggles.

I ignore her and stand quietly next to the back door.

"Shhh." I press my ear against the wood. When I hear noises coming from inside, I am thrilled and terrified at the same time. My chest starts pounding and a surge of adrenaline rushes through my veins. My thoughts start spinning out of control, and my feet feel like they need to run for miles before they can calm down. "This is it. *He* is in there."

"Who?"

"The freak who stole those black truffles. The crazy person who killed Professor Sellers. This is the only available kitchen on campus right now. If anything fishy is going on, it's happening *here*." I reach for the door handle, but Bree stops me.

"Are you crazy?" I hear her swallow hard. "Why don't we call the cops?"

"Because," I protest. "I might never get a chance like this again, and whoever is in there might leave at any moment. I have to at least see who it is, Bree."

She gulps and takes a step back. I nod at her, and she nods at me. My hand slowly turns the door knob. It is unlocked. My hands and feet feel prickly as I open the door. Light floods the sidewalk. I take a step inside, and immediately something hits my ankle. I jump and look down.

"Cole?" I gasp.

"Poppy," he says through his teeth. "Get *out* of here." He has a worried look on his face. My eyes dart around the kitchen. I look back at Cole and quickly realize that he has been tied to a chair. He rocks back and forth trying to scoot himself closer to the exit. His forehead looks damp, and there are sweat stains underneath the armpits of his shirt. I get down on my hands and knees and hide behind a counter. "*Poppy*." Cole rolls his eyes as he watches me crouch down and investigate instead of run to get help.

"Shhh." I glance back at the back door and it closes before Bree has the chance to follow me. I am alone now. I hear more noises. Pots and pans are clanging, and I hear sizzling from the deep fryers. Footsteps approach. I crawl to a corner as someone in an apron comes to retrieve more mixing bowls.

Hiking boots.

Faded jeans.

Blond hair.

Jeff.

A wave of disappointment washes over me when I see Jeff collecting mixing bowls like it is an everyday chore. All the while, Cole is tied up in the corner with a scowl on his face. My feeling of disappointment quickly turns to anger as I think about how he conned me into thinking he was a normal guy from Seattle with similar hopes and dreams as me. I jump to my feet, letting my emotions do my thinking. It's a habit that I can't shake.

"Hey!" I shout.

"Poppy!" Cole scolds me.

"Poppy?" Jeff responds, turning around. He raises his eyebrows. "You can't be here. Get out!"

"I'm not going anywhere until you tell me what's going on." I stamp my foot. Cole clears his throat. "Oh, and you let Cole go."

"Last chance," Jeff mutters. "Leave the way you came!"

"What's that, my boy?" another voice calls from across the kitchen. Heavy footsteps thud towards me. Mr. Harris steps forward. His forehead looks shiny in the light, and he practically growls when he sees me. His gaze is fiery, like a mad man lurks behind his eyes. "Grab her."

As soon as he commands it, Jeff grabs me. I struggle against his force, but he's too strong. He grips my arms so tight that I can start to feel bruises forming on my skin in the shape of his fingers. He grabs some butcher's string, the kind used to tie rotisserie chickens. With my hands behind my back, he ties me to the leg of a metal counter.

"I'm really sorry," Jeff says quietly. "But I *did* warn you." I try to jerk myself away from him, but I can't, so I settle for giving him a death glare. Jeff sighs and resumes with his chores. He returns to the nearest counter and begins grabbing more kitchen equipment for Mr. Harris.

"We'll decide what to do with them when we are done," Mr. Harris grunts. He wipes his forehead with his plump finger. I notice a Band-Aid wrapped around his thumb. He grabs one of the school's specially-made mixing bowls. I remember them from orientation. They have the school's emblem on them.

I watch Jeff mix a blend of spices, molasses, and sugar, and quickly catch on to the fact that he's making beignet batter. My eyes dart to a bowl of confectioner's sugar near the fryers. Each batch that Jeff completes is taken over to Mr. Harris for examining. I look at Cole.

"What are you doing here?" I mutter.

"I was on my way to scope out the crime scene when I saw Jeff out by the Dumpsters," he whispers.

"What happened to going together? We waited for you."

"I thought I would check to see if the coast was clear," he whispers back. "Being stealthy isn't really your strong suit. No offense."

"You realize what's happening here, don't you?"

"Late night snack attack?" Cole mutters.

"No." I say it a little too loud. Jeff turns around and looks at me. I refuse to make eye contact with him. I soften my voice. "No. Jeff and Mr. Harris were the ones making those strange noises in the student kitchens this whole time. They were the ones in the kitchen that night when we found Professor Sellers. *One* of them killed the professor."

"Professor Sellers must have walked in on them that night," he responds. "But why would they *kill* him? What's so incriminating about a late night beignet binge?"

I remember what James said back in Alabama. They have been making beignets since the school opened. Thomas Calle got into a fight with one of the teachers when he walked in on him making these sweet treats. Professor Sellers caught Jeff and Mr. Harris in the act and wound up dead.

"*Black truffles,*" I mutter out loud.

"What?" Cole tries shaking the chair to loosen his ropes. He does it a second time and starts wiggling his arms. Jeff hears him and races over with a kitchen knife. My entire body freezes with fear. Jeff glances at me and quickly cuts Cole's ropes.

"What are you—"

"Go," he instructs him. Jeff runs to cut me free. I feel relieved when the string around my arms and wrists finally drops to the floor. "The old man is crazy. Get out while you still can."

"You don't have to tell me twice," Cole says.

"What about you?" My chest is pounding so loudly that it is all I can hear.

"I have to stay," Jeff whispers. "Mr. Harris will turn me in if I don't."

"Turn you in for what?"

Cole pulls my arm towards the door with a pleading look on his face.

"I kind of lied on my school application," he admits.

"You *murdered* a man just so you wouldn't get kicked out of pastry school?" My face feels like it's on fire.

"Poppy," he barks. "I had nothing to do with that. I wasn't even there that night."

"And I am just supposed to take your word for it?" I reply.

"Alright," Mr. Harris yells. The sound of his voice scares me so much that it forces the air from my lungs. Heavy footsteps race in my direction. "Play time is over." I hardly have the chance to think before the back door bursts open. Detective Reid enters with a group of policemen and draws his gun as a sweaty, lumpy arm wraps around my waist. I hear Mr. Harris's nasally breathing in my ear, and it grosses me out. My entire spine fills with goose bumps. This might be the one time in my life I wish I wasn't so thin and petite. Mr. Harris grabs me with little effort, as if I'm a mini cupcake.

"Poppy, are you okay?" Detective Reid says calmly. He gently takes a step forward. I see Bree standing behind him. She's staring right at me and nervously biting her nails. I glance down and notice that Mr. Harris doesn't only have his disgusting, hairy arm around me. He is also holding up a kitchen knife, taking me as his hostage.

"What do *you* think?" I angrily respond.

"Let her go, professor." Detective Reid takes another step. He reaches out a hand like he's a long lost friend. "We can talk this out."

I hear Mr. Harris's breath quicken. His knuckles lock in place. He is starting to panic.

"Don't make another decision you'll regret later," the detective says firmly. He stares straight at him.

"I…I didn't," Mr. Harris stutters.

"I know," the Detective responds. He takes another step. "You didn't mean for any of this to happen."

I feel something moist drop onto my neck. I slowly look down, praying that it isn't blood. It is a tear. Another one drops onto my T-shirt. I feel Mr. Harris's grip around my waist start to loosen.

"It was an accident," he stammers. "I thought he was unconscious, not *dead*. He was only supposed to *forget* what he saw. He couldn't *know*. No one can *know*." He lets go of me to wipe his face.

A surge of adrenaline pumps through me, and I run as far from him as I can manage. My legs carry me towards the tray of warm beignets and I stumble, nearly knocking the whole pan over. A couple of warm beignets fall off the counter and break as they hit the floor. Something round and dark pokes out of the middle. I lean in closer to try and make out what it might be.

I hear the clicking of handcuffs as Detective Reid recites Mr. Harris his rights. Bree and Cole call my name, but I pick up a broken beignet and pick it apart. My nails hit something hard embedded in the center. I finish pulling apart the pastry and see a black lump in the center of the fried batter. I wipe away the mess of powdered sugar dusted on top and hold up a black truffle, added after the batter was fried and cooled.

"Yes!" I shout. "That's it."

"What is *that*?" Detective Reid asks. Bree and Cole stare at it looking bewildered. Mr. Harris hangs his head.

"One of the missing black truffles," I answer. I look at Jeff and remember how he carefully filled a box of hand-picked beignets for a couple of out-of-towners. "He has been selling the truffles by hiding them in these stupid beignets." The detective looks at Mr. Harris and then at Jeff. "How long has this tradition been going on, huh? Since the day the school opened?"

"Please," Mr. Harris says through his teeth. "Don't stain the reputation of this school with your silly accusations."

I glare at Jeff. He uncomfortably looks down at his shoes as he folds his arms.

"Jeff," I call him out. He takes a deep breath.

"Mr. Harris blackmailed me into making sure the goods were placed into the right hands," Jeff says, hanging his head. "Just like he did to Tom Fox before he ran off to get away from his mistakes."

I think back to the missing student poster that I saw on my first day. Tom Fox *did* run away, but not because the program was too much for him. It was his extracurriculars that nearly killed him.

"If that's true," Detective Reid responds. "*You* will have to come with me as well."

"I'll cuff him for you," Cole comments, scowling in Jeff's direction.

"Quiet," Bree says, hitting his arm.

As Mr. Harris and Jeff are escorted out, my heart gradually starts to slow down. I take a few calming breaths and shake my head at the pile of fresh beignets on the counter. Detective Reid walks towards me. His chiseled jaw is clenched. I look at his slacks and autumn orange tie, remembering Bree's comment about his looks.

"Well done," he says.

I laugh.

"Sounds like you almost had it figured out yourself," I reply. I bite the side of my lip and try not to stare at his face for too long. "You never thought I was guilty, did you?"

"No." He chuckles. "This place has gotten a mountain of theft reports since Mr. Dixon took over. I guess he's not in the loop."

"Right." I nod. "Well, you could have just said that."

"I wasn't sure I could trust you." His eyes lock with mine for a brief moment.

"And now?" I ask him.

"We'll see," he jokes. His hand lightly brushes my arm as he reaches for a bowl on the counter. He holds it up and studies the school's emblem engraved on it. The shape matches the indentation that was on Professor Sellers's head. I blink a few times trying to get his pale face and bruised head out of my mind.

"The murder weapon?" I ask. "He must have hit him pretty hard."

Detective Reid nods.

"I'm going to need *all* of these."

"Mr. Harris has a cut on his thumb, so one of these bowls probably has DNA matching both the victim and the suspect."

"Impressive." He grins and reaches into his pocket, pulling out his business card. "If anything else comes to mind."

"Yeah," I respond. "I will give you a call."

"In the meantime…" He looks around the kitchen at the mess that Mr. Harris made, starting with the burnt batter in the fryers and extending all the way across the kitchen where powdered sugar is dusted across the counters. "My team has a lot of work to do." Detective Reid promptly puts on a pair of gloves and begins the tedious task of tracking down every single kitchen item with the school's emblem engraved on it.

That's a whole lot of bowls.

CHAPTER SIXTEEN

———

The holiday break could not have come sooner. I get off the airplane and breathe in the Oregon air. I smell coffee. Lots of coffee. I pass a handful of coffee shops as I walk to the baggage claim to meet my mom. I find myself taking long, deep breaths as I pull my carry-on bag past security.

I see my mom waiting with a paper sack that I hope is filled with our Christmastime tradition of pumpkin spice muffins. Sometimes she makes them. Sometimes she buys them from our local bakery. Either way they taste amazing every time. I walk faster when I see her. Her thin frame is dressed in jeans and a red trench coat with brown hiking boots.

"I thought you would be hungry," she says, handing me the sack. My stomach rumbles.

"Yes," I respond. "Pumpkin spice. I love the holidays." I don't wait a minute before I bite into a muffin and let the sweet spices take me back to a Christmas morning when I was twelve and Grandma Liz gave me a blue, sparkly tutu that she sewed herself.

"It's nice to have you home again." She puts her arm around me and escorts me outside to the parking lot. It doesn't matter how old I am. I think Mom still sees me as a ten-year-old girl. Even if I walked off the plane carrying my own baby, she would still see me as a ten-year-old.

"How's my old apartment?" I ask.

"New renters moved in last month," she responds. "Your dad took care of all the details."

"Thanks." I haven't slept in my old room in years.

"How is school going so far?" she asks, running her fingers through her long, dark hair.

I knew both my parents would ask me this, and I have contemplated what to say to them. My dad already told me that pastry school wasn't the practical choice to make. I don't want to give him a reason to complain some more.

I know I should have stayed on the familiar route and moved into a career that was dance related, but I didn't want to. I wanted to start over. Grandma Liz would have understood. I tuck a strand of hair behind my ear and smile.

"It's going well." And now that the truffle killer has been caught, school really is going well for me. I feel like a weight has been lifted off my shoulders. That baker's rut I found myself in is slowly starting to dissolve. "I'll have to make you something."

"Nothing buttery," Mom comments. "Your father and I are on a vegan kick."

"Dairy-free," I say quietly. "I accept the challenge." I remember my *dieting* days, and how I used to get mad at myself for dreaming of doughnuts and flaky croissants. I would go days on nothing but dry chicken salads with no dressing. And it wasn't even the dark meat that I like. It was the boring breast meat. Less fat.

"You should try it out for a few days." She looks me up and down. "Maybe it will help you out with some of that puffiness."

"It's not puffiness. It's five extra pounds." My mother commenting about my weight is nothing new to me. I know it would bother some people, but it doesn't bother me. When you live the life of a professional ballerina having your body scrutinized is part of the territory. I realized as soon as I bit into one of Bree's sugary morsels that I would probably gain some weight while I was away at school.

"*Five?*"

"It's pastry school, Mom. It was bound to happen." I am already starting to regret not getting a hotel room.

"Well." She wrinkles her nose. "Just be careful when you go back."

"You mean try not to let anymore doughnut holes jump into my mouth?" I joke. She looks at me curiously. She doesn't find my comment funny. Lucky for her, I think I'll steer clear of beignets for a while.

I follow my mom to her car and put my bag in the trunk. I feel my phone buzz in my pocket. I smile when I see Cole's name on the screen. I read his text as we wait in line to pay for parking.

Cole: *How's Mom and Dad?*

Me: *Eh...at least I can breathe here.*

Cole: *Mama drama?*

Me: *The usual.*

Cole: *Are you going to practice your napoleons?*

Me: *Idk. The fam has gone vegan.*

Cole: *More for you then.*

Me: *I miss Bree's caramel filled cake balls.*

Cole: *Is that all you miss?*

I look up from my phone when heavy raindrops hit the windshield. Around me is familiar scenery, but I feel more like a visitor than an Oregon native. I miss Cole and my crazy roomie. I wonder what both of them are doing right now. Cole is probably grilling something at his aunt's house, and Bree is most likely back in Connecticut shopping for ingredients at her local market.

"Who's that?" my mom asks. She shakes her head. "Sorry, old habit. That's none of my business."

"A friend from Georgia." I smile. Cole still believes in my napoleons even though they suck. I laugh, quietly imagining him biting into a napoleon with flat puff pastry dough and lumpy cream. He would eat the whole thing to avoid hurting my feelings even if it was awful. "Mom, do you remember those candies that Grandma Liz used to make with me?"

"Brigadeiro," she responds. "Oh, I haven't had one of those in years."

"Me neither." I remember biting into one of those chocolaty truffles and feeling like I floated up to heaven for a few seconds. Grandma made me wait all day to have one. I would practically inhale my dinner just to be allowed a taste. Green vegetables included. "What if I made a batch?"

"Really?" She pauses for a minute. "Well, pumpkin, if you made *that* then I would eat it."

"Good." *Because I'll be making a whole lot more than just one batch.*

I take a deep breath and look back at my cell phone. I re-read Cole's last text. *Is that all you miss?* The real answer to that question is more characters than my phone will allow. The truth is I miss a lot of things.

Grandma's candy.

Sunday morning lattes before weekend rehearsals.

The cupcakery in NYC.

My pre-injury ballet body.

And I never realized it until now, but I miss sleuthing around CPA with my zany classmates. A new chapter of my life is starting, and I can't wait to return to my *beige* apartment and find Bree trying to perfect peppermint bark or Cole arguing about how mayo is better than Miracle Whip.

My fingers type a response to Cole's question.

A simple two-letter answer.

Me: *No.*

Cole: *;)*

CHAPTER SEVENTEEN

———

My childhood home sits at the top of a steep hill. It's an older house surrounded by trees and wildflowers. The backyard faces a lot of land covered in woods and wildlife. It was never cleared out to make space for more houses. It's too wild to tame now. I used to go exploring back there when I was little. I came across a giant toad once. I named him Fatso and kept him in the sink of my playhouse.

The sky is gray, and the air feels moist, but not the same way it feels in Georgia. It feels like mist is continually washing over me. Mom pulls up the driveway and gets out of the car. I grab my suitcase and follow her up the front, wooden steps. The inside of the house used to be a pea green color before Mom had it painted white a few years ago. She had also traded all her antique sofas for a set that was simpler and more modern. The only things left in this house that haven't changed are my brother's and my bedrooms.

"Wow," I say as I walk into the kitchen. "New floors?"

The kitchen cabinets used to be oak, but those were also painted white to match the rest of the house. Through the window above the sink you can see the woods in the backyard. Above the kitchen table is a skylight. Though the sun is hidden behind rain clouds at the moment, the white walls against the immense amount of green outside have a way of brightening up the room.

"No more linoleum," she happily responds.

My dad is tall, thin, and dark-haired like the rest of my family. He sits at the kitchen table reading a newspaper. A warm mug of tea is steaming next to him. He looks up and grins.

"Poppy," Dad greets me. "Welcome back."

"Can I get you something, honey?" My mom opens a cupboard and pulls out a mug.

"Coffee?"

"Oh, we've switched to tea." She glances at Dad. "It's healthier."

"Right." I nod.

"Tea is fine." I set my suitcase aside and sit next to Dad at the table. It feels strange to walk into a room and not have an AC unit blasting or a fan circulating some sort of breeze. Even though it's technically wintertime, it still feels hot in Georgia. The sun doesn't beat down on me like it did during the summer, but the air is still warm and simple outdoor walks always make me feel sweaty.

"You look different," my dad comments. "Is it your hair?"

"Dan," my mom scolds him. "Our daughter is a *curvy* type of girl now. Don't make a big deal of it."

My dad raises his eyebrows and resumes reading his paper. I watch my mom pull out a tea bag and steep it in some hot water. She opens another cupboard to retrieve a box of vegan biscuits. She places a couple on a small dessert plate and places them in front of me. They look like circles of cardboard compared to the stuff that Bree makes.

"Thanks," I say quietly.

"I hope you don't mind green tea?" My mom hands me a mug and sits next to me. "It's good for your metabolism."

"Of course."

Her eyes crinkle when she smiles at me. I know she is only trying to help, but she's making it feel like a sin to enjoy a round, fat buttery shortbread cookie. I reluctantly taste the vegan biscuit. It tastes a little like seaweed.

"Good, aren't they?" My mom nods as if they are sugary morsels that I should love just as much as she does. "Well, if you're going to make us all something you should probably head on to the store."

"Now?" I glance at Dad as he crosses his legs and turns the page, staring intently at the headline at the top. "It's just us three. I'm sure I can work with ingredients that you already have and make something small."

"Oh, did I forget to mention that your brother will be here later today?"

"Yes." My eyes go wide. "You *did* forget to mention that."

"Yeah, he'll be here around the same time as your Aunt Maggie and Uncle George."

"What?"

"Yes, for our annual, family holiday party tonight," Mom responds.

"You didn't tell me that that was tonight." My parents throw a holiday party for everyone on our street every year. Last year I flew in from New York and stayed with my ex. The two of us mostly fooled around in my old bedroom the entire night. Mom usually hires a Santa to come, and we all take family pictures. Back when all the kids on our block were younger, Mom would set up some sort of cookie decorating station, but lately there haven't been any children in attendance. The cookie station quickly turned into a spot to store more booze.

"Yes, I've hired someone to take care of the food this year."

"All vegan?" I add.

"Mostly." She sits up straight in her chair and smoothes a piece of her dark hair.

"So we aren't having a turkey this year? Or any of that gingerbread fudge that Grandma used to make?"

"Tofurky is just as good," she responds. She's glancing outside, cupping her mug like it contains liquid chocolate. I roll my eyes. *Tofurky?* If Bree were here she would explode. She would march right down to the nearest grocery store, buy up all the fat they had in stock, and start filling the house with sweets until my parents couldn't take it anymore.

I would give that a try, but I am pretty sure my mom would fall over and have a heart attack if she saw that much butter and lard all in one place. Like me, she is naturally thin, but she can take dieting to extremes sometimes. I used to be like that. Crazy about food. I still am crazy about food, but in a different way. I let it brighten my day, not rule it.

"Mom, you can't serve everyone Tofurky."

"They won't even know the difference," she laughs. "I don't anymore, and your father says he loves it."

I glance at my dad, but he avoids making eye contact.

"It's tofu," I say. "They will see and taste the difference, trust me."

Mom shrugs. Once she has made up her mind she doesn't change it. I gulp down the rest of my green tea, pretending it is a pumpkin spice latte with a shot of espresso, and stand up. I grip the handle of my suitcase and head into the family room and towards the staircase. I notice that Mom has already put up her Christmas tree. At least *that* still looks the same. The Christmas balls are royal blue and silver just like when I was little.

I walk upstairs into my tiny bedroom. It's a little smaller than my room at Calle Pastry Academy, but I have my own bathroom. The walls are painted a light, ballerina pink, and there's a twin bed in the corner with a black-and-white comforter. The components of my room clash together, sharing two personalities. The black-and-white, bold patterns from my high school days, joined with the pink from my younger years when I thought fairies lived on my windowsill.

I set my luggage down and sit on my bed, looking up at the ceiling. I haven't had much time to think about the past couple weeks because they flew by so fast. After Mr. Harris was arrested, Jeff disappeared from classes for a few days. He eventually returned but had avoided me ever since. Understandable. I didn't exactly smile at him the first time we made eye contact. I was still too upset.

President Dixon apologized for the trouble I'd been through and made sure the entire staff knew I had nothing to do with Professor Sellers' death or the truffle theft. He gave the whole school a day off to attend the memoriam, and one of the senior classes submitted a new recipe to the student bakery for them to start selling in memory of him. Kiwi cheesecake. Apparently, it was his favorite. There was a lot about him that I didn't know or understand.

I suppose no matter how much we disliked each other, one thing we did have in common was a love of desserts.

* * *

It's a weird feeling when you visit your hometown grocery store and see people working there whom you went to high school with. I see a guy, who I am pretty certain used to be in algebra with me, stacking tomatoes. I duck into the baking aisle to avoid an awkward hello. My fingers run along the selection of baking chocolate.

I decided to make Grandma Liz's chocolate candies and an amazing vegan dessert to prove to Mom and Dad that I'm serious about pastry school. I've never made a dairy-free dessert, but who can say no to chocolate? I pick out a few different brands of baking chocolate and move on to the cocoa powders.

"I don't know what I'm doing," I say out loud. I glance down at my heels, thinking about the fact that I have nothing to wear to the party tonight. It doesn't matter though, because this year I'm dateless. I reach into my purse and pull out my cell phone. I dial someone who might be able to help me with at least *one* of my dilemmas.

"Hello?" a voice says on the other line.

"Bree," I respond, glaring at a bag of white chocolate chips. "Have you ever made a dairy-free cake before?"

"Hello to you too." I hear her giggle. "Already missing the South? You should come visit me in Connecticut sometime. You really won't want to leave after you do."

"My parents have gone *vegan*."

"No," she gasps.

"And I need to impress them at our holiday party tonight. Please tell me you can help."

She pauses for a moment.

"I have made a gluten-free, dairy-free chocolate cake before, but it was a little tricky."

"Let's hear it," I eagerly reply. "What do I need?"

"For starters, grab some dark chocolate. *Don't* use milk chocolate. I made that mistake once, and my old boss Ms. Neriwether almost had my head for it."

"Dark chocolate," I respond. "Check."

"You *can* use cake flour," she says. "But you can also use nut flour or black bean flour."

I wrinkle my nose.

"Maybe for my first time I'll just stick to regular cake flour."

"So holiday party, you say? You mean like a *Christmas* party?"

"No." I correct her. "One of our neighbors is Jewish so my mom makes sure everyone knows it's a *holiday* party."

"No eggnog then?" Bree responds.

"Who knows?" I grab a few more ingredients and place them in my basket. "She's having the party catered this year which is a little strange. She always makes everything herself. Sometimes with my help."

"Maybe it's a special one?"

"I don't know," I answer. "I mean my older brother is coming into town, so maybe that's it? He wasn't able to make it last year because he couldn't pull himself away from work. He's works at an investment firm in Boston."

"Uh-huh." I hear her take a deep breath, and it makes me take a step back from the candy aisle and wait for what she has to say next.

"What?"

"Oh nothing," she says quietly.

"No," I insist. "What aren't you saying? I know you have an opinion about this. You always do."

"It's just that this sounds an awful lot like the one time my cousin came to visit from London. My aunt threw a huge party and...well, he came to tell us all that he got married."

"Married?" I nearly choke on my own spit. "Oh, please. Mark doesn't have time for a relationship. He barely had time for me, and we only lived four hours away from each other."

"Well to be fair, four hours is a long way to drive."

"Sure," I mutter into the phone. "Take his side."

"I never thought I would have to say this to a friend, but the holidays will be over before you know it."

"I guess all I can hope for is a kick-ass cake," I reply.

"Yes." She takes another deep breath. "A kick-*butt* cake."

* * *

Making brigadeiro in my parent's kitchen brings back lots of warm memories. My hands move on their own as I melt all the ingredients together in a pot and stir quickly. I used to stand on a chair and watch Grandma Liz do this. I expect this is the way James feels when he makes his dad's southern peach pie back in Alabama. It's easy, and it's enjoyable.

My mom tugs at the string of my apron when she walks by. I glance at her before pouring the hot candy mixture onto a marble cutting board. It needs to cool just long enough for me to roll the mixture into balls and dip them in chocolate jimmies. The kitchen timer chirps, and I check my dark chocolate vegan cake. The smell of it escapes into the kitchen as I open the oven. My mom pauses and takes a second whiff as I pull the cake out of the oven.

"Honey, that smells amazing."

"It's vegan," I inform her.

She nods her head looking impressed. Her eyes dart from my cake to Grandma's candies to my evergreen knit sweater. She gently touches the material as if she's sizing it up at a department store.

"You'd better go and change," she suggests. "The caterers have just arrived, and I expect your brother any minute now."

"Mom, it's only a sweater." I touch the candy mixture and grab a ball of it with my fingers. It's still a little too hot, but I begin forming balls of candy and dunking them in a bowl of chocolate jimmie sprinkles. I also set aside another bowl with red and green sprinkles.

"But honey, you want to make a good first impression." She turns her head as a couple of men carrying white boxes enter the kitchen and begin setting up the food.

"What do you suggest I wear then?"

"I don't know?" She casually tilts her head. "A *dress* maybe?"

"High heels, yes. But a dress—"

"Just wear one," she instructs me. I haven't even been here a day, and already I'm back to being the little girl who didn't clean her room. "You'll thank me. I promise."

I raise my eyebrows and roll a couple more candy balls. I place them on a Christmas serving platter that I found in a box under the stairs. Before I have time to ask my mom what's going on, she leaves the room. I sigh and finish preparing my desserts. I set the Christmas dish aside and jog up to my room to look for something more suitable to wear.

I look through my old closet and a box of clothes that I left here before I went to Georgia. I pull out a silky maroon dress that I wore to a Broadway play once back in NYC. It cinches at the waist and puffs out a little around the hips. It is short, but I also find a pair of black tights and heels to go with it. The neckline fits differently than I remember when I slip the dress on. I guess some of those five pounds found their way to my chest.

I glance in the mirror, pleased with what I see. The feeling is new to me. I'm looking in the mirror without scrutinizing my appearance. I don't have rehearsals to worry about and calories to count. I can just be myself now. I'm not ashamed of the fact that I am going to eat *two* pieces of cake and hide a few of Grandma's candies so I can indulge in them later when everyone goes home. Maybe I'll even sneak in a little contraband while I'm at it. *Coffee.*

The doorbell rings, and I listen to Mom race to the front door. She greets my brother as soon as she answers it. My eyes go wide when I hear the sound of a second person. A *female*. My big brother, Mark, brought a date.

I finish getting myself ready and peek over the banister trying to get a view of his new girlfriend. I see Mark in a tailored, navy blue suit. His dark hair is perfectly gelled, and he's holding the hand of a blonde woman whose face I cannot see. Chills run down my spine when the woman flicks her hair over her shoulder. It reminds me of Georgina.

"Oh honey," Mom calls me from upstairs. "Come on down. I can't believe my two babies are so grown up now."

My cheeks feel warm as I casually stroll down the staircase in my fancier getup. I act as if I'd been planning to come downstairs all along. I plan each step carefully, hoping that I don't get a stroke of bad luck and trip and fall. Mark looks surprised when he turns towards me. He and I were close once, but ever since he left for college all those years ago the two of us had grown apart.

"Poppy," Mark says. He leans in and gives me a side hug. "When Mom said you were baking muffins down in swamp country I thought she was kidding. But I see you came to your senses." He grins and looks at his date.

"Actually, I'm on my holiday break."

"Oh," he responds, briefly glancing down at his loafers.

"Um, Poppy, nice to meet you. I'm Lauren." Mark's date outstretches her hand. She's wearing a winter blue cocktail dress, and her coat is long and white. I smile politely and shake her hand. My eyes dart to her fair and fragile fingers. No wedding ring.

"Yeah," I respond.

The doorbell rings.

"I'll get it," Mom says. She opens the front door, letting in my Aunt Maggie and Uncle George. A few neighbors, ones that I don't know, walk up. The house begins filling up with guests, and I'm relieved that there are more people to talk to besides Mark and his new date.

"Excuse me," I say, leaving the room. I look over my shoulder and see Lauren nudge my brother in the stomach. I walk into the kitchen where the food is being laid out on the kitchen table. Mom wasn't kidding when she said that she and Dad were on a vegan kick. The Tofurky is displayed in the center of trays of vegetables. I see a couple of salads, fruit, and a quinoa dish. It doesn't look bad, but it's nothing compared to the hearty spread at Shurbin Farms. There are no warm buttery rolls or creamed collard greens.

The doorbell rings again, and this time I hear Mom shout my name.

"No way," a voice says near the entryway. "Poppy, is that you?" My childhood friend Evie walks towards me and gives me a hug.

"Evie," I respond. "I haven't seen you in—"

"Four years," she finishes. "Wow, look at you."

"I know." I look down at my dress. "I'm not as slender as I once was but—"

"I think you look great," she interrupts. She tucks a strand of her auburn hair behind her ear and nods. Her eyes dart to the food on the kitchen table. "Quite a spread."

"You know you're the first person to compliment me since I've been back." I fold my arms. "I think my mom is convinced I'm having a midlife crisis."

"Oh, the whole pastry school thing?" Evie takes a closer look at the food. She almost picks up a cherry tomato and pops it in her mouth.

"You know too?"

"My mom told me about it." She directs her attention to me again and chuckles to herself. "But don't dwell on it. I think pastry school is a brilliant idea."

"Really?" I stand up straighter. "Where were you when I was talking about applying?"

"Well, think of it this way." She tugs at the collar of her emerald green dress. It makes her look sophisticated, and I would expect nothing less from a Rocky Mountain journalist. "You spent your twenties doing something you were good at."

"*Mediocre*," I comment.

"And now you get to spend your thirties doing something you *love*. You've always been obsessed with food. Whether or not you ate it, you were always obsessed with it."

"I still am." I look into the living area and tiptoe quietly to the Christmas dish I set aside. I hold it up and let her study the perfectly formed Brazilian truffles on the plate. Her eyes go wide, and unlike that cherry tomato, she grabs one like they're about to go extinct. She smells it before she puts it in her mouth.

"Are these what I think they are?" She takes a huge bite. "Yes, they are!"

The doorbell rings again, bringing in more chatter to the living area. The house is progressively getting louder and louder. My mom steps into the kitchen. She studies my outfit before she nods and looks over my shoulder.

"Poppy," Mom says firmly. "You have a guest." She stands aside, and a man in a gray blazer with dirty blond hair steps past her. My entire torso feels like a tub of frozen ice cream. I haven't spoken this man's name since we broke up.

"Mom?" My head is starting to spin. I don't know what to do first. Yell at my mother for letting him into the house or kick my ex-boyfriend out the door before I accidentally strangle him.

"Now Poppy," Mom states. "I know you two broke up, but Locke started his own business, and I really think you two should talk."

"Oh dear Lord," Evie murmurs.

"Poppy." When my ex says my name like that, my feelings for him come pouring back. That's the problem with toxic relationships like ours. All I have to do is think about him, and I start thinking of nothing else. That's why I haven't even allowed myself to say his name out loud.

"Locke." I swallow the lump in my throat.

"I think we should talk."

"I should probably go," Evie comments, snagging another piece of candy.

"No, Evie, I think you should stay." I snatch her sleeve so she can't leave.

"Come on, Poppy." He sighs and places a hand in his coat pocket. "Don't be like this."

"Yep." Evie jerks herself away. "I'm outtie."

Evie leaves the kitchen along with the rest of the caterers. Locke and I are left alone while the sounds of laughter and shuffling feet ring through the house, covering up the dead silence between us. I don't know what Locke has to say to me, but I know it can't be good. Locke isn't only my ex-boyfriend, he's my addiction. And just when I think I'm clean he shows up out of nowhere.

"I'll meet you upstairs," he says with a wink.

CHAPTER EIGHTEEN

———

I will have to go upstairs to my room eventually. Locke is in there waiting, and the thought of being alone with him in my room makes my stomach churn. I would rather take my chances chatting with my brother's date, Lauren. I nervously watch the grandfather clock in the living room, as my Aunt Maggie gives me a hug and tells me about my cousin Sam traveling across Thailand.

I nod every couple of seconds, but I'm barely listening to a word she is saying. Instead, I think of what I'm going to say to my ex. He wants me back. That part is obvious. But do I want *him* back? Maybe he really has changed. Gotten his life together. Stopped making frequent trips to that disgusting gentlemen's club.

No, Poppy. He's the same old Locke. He will never change.

"Oh, would you look at that," Aunt Maggie points out. "Your mother forgot to put out plates and silverware. I should go see if she needs any help with that." She gently squeezes my forearm and leaves.

I look at each step until I'm watching the top of the stairs to see if Locke changed his mind. My bedroom door is cracked slightly open. I bite the corner of my lip as I reluctantly walk up the staircase. More neighbors walk through the front door, and now the living room is so chaotic that no one notices me leaving.

I push open my bedroom door and see Locke waiting for me on my bed. My heart starts pounding as I remember all the things we'd done together in this very room. By the smirk on his face, I know he is thinking the same thing. He stands up, taking a step closer so I can smell his woodsy cologne. His dirty blond hair isn't as messy as I remember it, and he looks like a confident businessman in his blazer and fitted jeans.

"Poppy." His voice is deep. It's one of things that attracted me to him from the start.

"Locke." My voice quivers. I bite my lip even harder to keep myself from sounding anxious.

"It's been a while," he continues.

"So it has."

He takes another step.

"We have a lot of catching up to do." He leans in closer. My chest leaps as his warm hand touches my waist. Locke presses his lips against mine. His other hand caresses my cheek. I force myself to pull away. Kissing him again brings back too many memories. Good ones and bad ones.

But mostly bad ones.

"Locke," I scold him. "What are you doing? You and I aren't together anymore."

"Poppy." He doesn't look as concerned as me. "Let's leave the past in the past, okay? You went away, and I started my own consulting business, and now you're back. Let's just move on." He leans in to kiss me again, and though my heart is pounding and my extremities feel tingly, I don't let him this time.

"I'm not here to stay," I respond. "And you and I are done. For good."

"Look." Locke rolls his eyes. "You can't expect all your problems to go away by baking cookies and trading recipes or whatever it is you went off to do. I am talking about real life here."

"Pastry school *is* my life now." I feel tears forming behind my eyes. The pressure builds until I blink a few times, making my eyes moist and glassy. "It makes me happy. And think what you want, but I *will* be successful at it someday." I stand aside, gesturing towards the door. "Now get out."

Locke shakes his head, glaring at me like I'm the one who ruined our relationship. He always does this—finds ways to blame me for his mistakes. I can't live like that anymore, and for a whole semester at Calle Pastry Academy I didn't have to.

I miss the South.

"Unbelievable." Locke strolls into the hallway and chuckles lowly. "You know, the only reason I even came here tonight was because your mom told me you were having some kind of mental breakdown or something."

"What?"

"Or was it midlife crisis?" He shrugs. "But I guess I would be a mess too if my career was over and I had to start all over again." He raises his eyebrows and quickly jogs down the stairs before I can say anything in response.

I blink again, letting a tear escape. It runs down my cheek and drops off of my chin and onto my silk dress. The people who care about me are back in Georgia. The people who actually *want* me to succeed are miles and miles away. I wipe away my tear, thinking about my Grandma Liz and all the people who probably laughed at her when she decided to open her bakery.

She did it anyway, and so will I.

I compose myself and peek over the banister. The front door slams, and I see Locke's figure walking down the steep driveway. He's gone, and now I'm ready to take on anything. I walk down the staircase feeling like a new woman. I may not be a ballerina anymore, but I sure as hell can cook a mean peach pie. I am going to win that dessert contest, and I am going to do it with grandma's recipe.

"There you are." My mom meets me at the bottom of the staircase. "Your dad was just about to say a few words before everyone starts eating. Where is Locke?"

"He's gone, Mom."

"Oh," she sighs. "Well, be a dear and go grab my bell from the kitchen."

"Sure," I agree. It has always been tradition for my dad to say a few words about friends and family before the party starts. My mom then rings her Christmas bell, which she carefully labels a *holiday* bell when certain neighbors are present, and everyone moves into the kitchen to start eating.

I walk into the kitchen, admiring the setup on the table even though it's not Mom's traditional turkey this year. I place my vegan chocolate cake at the end of the table, hoping it will be an instant hit. I turn towards the window and see a hint of something strange outside by the garbage cans.

Jeans.

A flannel shirt.

Cowboy boots.

I quickly open the door leading into the backyard and step onto the moist grass. My heels sink into the mud. I fold my arms as a chill breeze gives me goose bumps. The man in front of me doesn't look startled that I caught him doing something shady in my backyard. He actually looks pleased. His weathered face and sun-burnt skin sends chills down my spine.

"*Dirk*?"

"Well, if it isn't Poppy Peters. How are you, ma'am?" He tilts his head as if he's wearing a cowboy hat. Out of all the people I met in the South, the head farm hand from Shurbin Farms is the last person I expect to see.

"What are you doing here?"

"One word," he breathes, "revenge."

The sky seems grayer when I look down and see raindrops hitting the windows on the side of the house. My shoulders feel cold and clammy as the rain falls heavier and heavier. Dirk's eyes dart to the trash cans and then back at me.

"What?" I shout over the sound of thunder. "What are you talking about?"

"You cost me a fortune," he huffs. His cheeks turn red. A fiery spark lights in his eyes when he takes a better look at my face. "All those years of planning and smuggling. We had the perfect operation going until you came along and ruined it all."

"Smuggling?"

He takes a step towards me, and I'm instantly enveloped in a bubble made up of fear and anxiety. The bubble begins to suffocate me. I can hardly breathe. It's like I have a stack of pastry-filled cake boxes sitting on top of my chest and no way to push them off.

"You are a bright one, aren't you?" he mocks me. "When you exposed our smuggling business, who did you think called all the shots, huh? Certainly not Mr. Harris and his student puppets. I knew we were in trouble when he insisted on blackmailing that brainiac Tom Fox into working for him, and then he ran off like a coward."

"So it was you this whole time?" I gulp.

"Why do you think Thomas Calle left the Academy all those years ago?" He chuckles, enjoying his opportunity to prove that I had it all wrong. That he had deceived me and it was easy. "He didn't run away. He was kicked out by his own father. *Shunned* for turning Calle Pastry Academy into the most profitable racket in all of Georgia. All those stories James told you in Alabama were lies invented by Thomas himself, except for the part about the kitchen fight."

"So Thomas Calle started a smuggling business to sell black market truffles via the student bakery?" I ask. "This is all about some fancy mushrooms?"

"Oh, wake up," he scoffs. "We smuggle anything and everything. As long as it fits into the goods, we sell it." He widens his shoulders and lifts his chin, looking down at me. "Thomas knew my father through some business dealings, and the two of them built this business together, no thanks to that French moron Francois. And now the business is all mine, and what do you do? You come in and stick your nose where it doesn't belong. Well, I'll show you what happens to youngins who stick their noses where they don't belong."

All the muscles in my body feel like they're flexing all at once as I bend down and grab the only weapon I can find. A rock from my mom's flowerbed. I hold it up as my wet locks fall across part of my face.

"Don't come any closer," I warn him. "I'll scream, and I'm a *really* loud screamer." I swallow the lump in my throat, hoping that someone has noticed that I'm outside in the pouring rain.

"I believe you," Dirk replies. He still has a smirk on his face, and it's killing me. Why hasn't he charged at me yet? Why isn't he pulling out a gun and waving it around in the air like a madman?

"Why didn't James just kill us when we came asking questions, huh?" I ask. "Why wait until now?"

"James isn't in on it. That's the best part." He throws his head back and laughs. "His dad never told him what he *really* did for a living. All the profit is mine, and mine alone. I don't need James anymore. I was days away from handing him my resignation."

"Save it for the cops," I shout, glancing again at the kitchen window. "And don't you even think about vandalizing my parents property or—"

"Sweetheart," he interrupts. "I'm afraid the damage has already been done. James will *never* find out about this, and you're not going to tell him." His expression changes to one that looks friendlier, but I still feel like I'm going to collapse at any moment. My hand is shaking, and my skin is starting to feel numb from the cold.

Dirk hops over the wood fence like it's made of cardboard. He has no problem maneuvering his body to the other side where his car is waiting. I hear his engine rev, and in seconds he speeds off. My hand finally drops the rock. I let out a giant yelp as I race to the garbage cans to see why Dirk found them so comical. I stand on my tiptoes and look over the side.

"Empty jugs?" I say out loud. "Empty jugs of…" I reach down and grab one of the empty containers. "Weed killer?"

I drop the container and glance back at the house. My eyes go wide when it finally dawns on me what Dirk came here to do. His plan for revenge didn't involve hurting just me. He came here to hurt all the people I care about. I turn too quickly and feel something in my back pop.

"Ah!" I automatically yell as a sharp tingle pierces my side. I take baby steps back to the house, keeping my shoulders and back hunched to avoid any extra pain. When I finally open the back door, I take a deep breath. I hear my dad speaking to all our guests in the living room.

They started the party without me. My fingers fumble and shake as I wring the water from my hair and dress. My tights feel like too damp clothes against my legs. I shake my dress as much as I can to prevent it from being see-through. I gasp when I catch my reflection in the glass window over the kitchen sink. My heavy mascara is running down my cheek, and I look like a hunchback in a transparent robe. Another needle-like pain pierces my back, but I focus my attention on the food.

Dirk must have poisoned the food.

What did he poison? What!

My eyes dart from the Tofurky to the many side dishes of sautéed vegetables. A platter of assorted nuts and a serving bowl of pumpkin curry soup are sitting beside them. I can't be certain what it was. I would have to taste everything to figure it out and even then I still won't know for sure until I see someone doubled over, puking on the porch.

There were a *lot* of empty containers in the trash. My heart starts pounding, and I take small steps towards the house phone to call the police. Mom is going to hate me for this, but I have to do it. The living room falls silent for a brief second.

"I was going to wait until later but..." My brother, Mark, takes the floor. I glance into the living room and see him reach into his jacket pocket. He pulls out a tiny box, and right away my mom gasps, covering her mouth with her hand. He gently kneels and looks at his date, Lauren. He slowly opens the box, revealing a glittering engagement ring. "Lauren, we've been friends for a while, and now that we're finally together I want to make *us* official. Will you marry me?"

The entire room gasps and patiently waits for Lauren's response. As soon as her eye catches the diamond on the ring, she starts nodding. I run my fingers through my wet hair and stand silently wondering what's going on in her head or if she even loves my brother at all.

"Yes," she answers. "Yes Mark, I will!" She leaps into his arms, and the entire room breaks out in applause. My mom's cheeks are rosy, and she doesn't waste any time hugging her new daughter-in-law to be.

"Oh my goodness," Mom says repeatedly. She studies Lauren's ring and turns to give my brother a smile of approval. "Well on that happy note, let's eat, everyone!"

The joyous crowd makes their way towards the kitchen. At least twenty hungry people are headed my way, and somehow I have to convince them not to touch a single thing on the table. I start to panic. My chest pounds and the pain in my back comes flooding back. I can hardly keep myself from howling like a wild animal.

Aunt Maggie walks in first, and behind her is an entire line of starving guests. She eyes a slice of cucumber on the vegetable platter and picks it up with her fingers. I lunge forward. She looks up and cringes when she sees my face.

"Oh dear," she says quietly. "Poppy, what happened to you?"

"Stop," I shout. "Don't eat that!"

Both my parents step into the kitchen along with Mark and his new fiancée. My mom looks at me like I'm a ghost who has come to haunt her nightmares. She turns towards the rest of her guests and tries to herd them away, but the entire bunch is too curious. More people push into the kitchen, including my old friend Evie.

"Honey, maybe you should go upstairs and lie down?" Mom suggests. But she scolds me with her eyes. "Go on."

"No," I reply. "I'm serious. You can't eat the food. No one can. Something's wrong with it."

"Oh," Mom laughs uncomfortably. "She's a little unnerved by the veganism." She turns to her guests, and continues laughing until others join her.

"No, Mom, I don't have a problem with veganism."

My Aunt Maggie looks at her cucumber slice and moves it towards her mouth. My throat tightens as I watch her, and I do the only thing I can think of to keep her from poisoning herself. I jump forward and knock the bit of food from her hand. My hand slaps against hers.

"Poppy!" Dad gasps. "What has gotten into you?"

"See, Dan." My mom points at me and looks back at my dad. "What did I tell you? She's cracked! We've been letting her fill her head with all these delusions, and she's finally gone mental!"

"Not here, Bobbi," Dad says through his teeth. "Our daughter is almost thirty years old."

"Exactly! She's about to be thirty years old and she has *no* career, *no* man in her life, and *no* hopes of giving us grandchildren." She throws her hands up in the air. If anyone in the room is going mental, it's my mom.

My chest keeps pounding, and my entire face feels like it's on fire. My Uncle George takes a step forward, practically ignoring the drama, and grabs a plate. He then proceeds to eye the food on the table. When he reaches for a handful of assorted nuts, more guests follow his lead. I roll my eyes.

"What do I have to do to get through to you people?" I say out loud.

I take a step forward and knock Uncle George's plate out of his hands. He stares at me, bewildered. The only way I can get everyone to forget about the food is to get rid of it all. I rub my forehead. What I'm about to do is not going to aid my plea that I'm not crazy.

I quickly grab the serving platter of Tofurky and drop it. The porcelain tray shatters, leaving lumps of tofu strewn across the tile. I do the same with every single dish on the table. As fast as I can, I dig into the food with my fingers and toss it on the floor or into the trash. *Anything* to make it look less appetizing.

I hear gasps and whispers, but I don't care. I'm doing them a favor even if I look like I just escaped from an insane asylum in the process. I throw the nut platter in the trash and scoop out handfuls of quinoa until the whole bowl is empty. I turn to my vegan cake. My pride and joy that I spent hours making just for the approval of my loon of a mother. I can't be sure that it's not contaminated somehow so I tear it apart.

"Poppy, stop this right now!" My mom places a hand on her chest as if she is about to have a heart attack.

I ignore her until every last morsel of food in the kitchen is in pieces on the floor. When I'm finished, I take a deep breath and finally look at everyone. Most of the faces I see are terrified. Some are concerned. And Evie is laughing in the corner.

"Um." I take a deep breath. "Sorry, everyone. I guess the party is cancelled."

It's for their own good.

"She's right." Evie clears her throat and begins pushing guests back into the living room. "Nothing to see here, people. Keep moving. Keep moving." She herds as many guests as she can until it is just me and my family standing in the kitchen. I fold my arms and attempt to cover the bits that can be seen through the fabric of my dress.

"Do you care to explain yourself?" Dad begins.

"Would you believe me if I said that someone poisoned the food?"

"Mark," Lauren says quietly, grabbing my brother's arm. "Maybe we should go."

"Yes," he agrees. He gives my mom a hug goodnight. "Night, Mom. We're going to head over to our hotel. I'll call you in the morning."

"Bye, sweetheart." My mom watches him leave. She looks down at the mess on the floor and avoids looking at me. "Well, I'll send everybody home." She stops just before the door leading to the living area and straightens her shoulders.

"Dad." I kick a piece of broccoli off my shoe. "I promise you I have a completely rational explanation for all this."

"Okay," he responds, hanging his head. "Let's hear it." My dad is more patient than my mom. I know he will at least give me the chance to explain, but I'll have to start at the beginning.

"Mind if I change first?"

Dad nods approvingly as I tiptoe upstairs and pull a set of warm pajamas from my suitcase. They were too warm to wear in Georgia. I quickly dry my hair with a towel and fish through my purse until I find the card Detective Reid gave me. I need proof that I'm not crazy.

I pull out my cell phone and dial his number.

It goes straight to his voice mail.

Beep.

"Hi, Detective Reid. It's Poppy Peters. Call me back as soon as you get this message. Mr. Harris isn't your *only* guy. Some crazy farmer just tried to kill me with a Tofurky."

CHAPTER NINETEEN

———

I take a sip of green tea as Detective Reid instructs his team to take samples of all the leftover food. My mom almost had a heart attack yesterday when I completely trashed the catered meal that she had paid so handsomely for. But what made her panic even more was hearing that she wasn't allowed to clean it up until the crime scene was properly assessed.

"You're a lucky woman, Mrs. Peters," Detective Reid informs my parents. "This could have turned out to be one deadly dinner party."

"I just hope you find the man responsible," she dramatically replies.

I get a kick out of watching her rub the side of her face and collapse onto the sofa like she's experiencing vertigo. When Detective Reid got my call, he immediately jumped on the next plane. He arrived this morning, confirming to my parents that I'm not a nut job and a psychotic farmhand really did try to poison us all out of spite.

"We've picked up his trail," the detective responds. "I've got all my best officers tracking him now. It won't be long before he makes another mistake."

"Thank you, Detective."

Detective Reid grins as he glances at me near the kitchen. I look down at my high-heeled boots and dark wash jeans. Here is a more appropriate place to wear them than in Georgia, where my feet sweat even in winter.

"First Mr. Harris and now this?" he says to me.

"We've got to stop meeting like this," I respond.

"At least now we know how far back this goes." He watches his team examine the food in the kitchen. After all the samples are collected, Detective Reid urges them to clean up a little while my mom searches for an aspirin for her headache.

"Since the school opened apparently."

He takes another look at the mess in the kitchen and glances at me.

"You really did all that?" he asks.

"Someone had to." I smile about the whole situation for the first time. "They would've eaten it all if I didn't, and we'd be having this conversation at a hospital."

"That was brave of you to make a fool of yourself like that."

"That's putting it lightly," I comment. "My neighbors think I've gone insane, and I single-handedly ruined what was supposed to *also* be my brother's engagement party. My mother had it all planned."

"I'm sorry." He offers his sympathy, but the damage has already been done. I explained everything to Mom and Dad. *Everything.* Down to the night Mr. Harris held me at knife point. My mom's first words were something along the lines of suing the school for nearly getting me killed. I disappointed her when I said I was going back after the break to finish what I started.

My dad was more understanding, but he's a man of few words. Unlike Mom, he usually chooses to keep his mouth shut and wait for a moment of privacy to speak his feelings. Mom doesn't understand privacy.

"It's okay," I lie, "I'm sure everyone will forget all about yesterday in a couple years…or decades."

* * *

Mark and his new fiancée were supposed to come over for dinner, but Mom couldn't bring herself to step into the kitchen after Detective Reid's team left. I took over and finished cleaning the mess I made even though my back was still a little sore from yesterday. I even scrubbed the tile floors on my hands and knees until it sparkled in the sunlight. That's when I looked up at the counters and realized that I had enough ingredients to make more of Grandma Liz's special Christmas candies, the Brazilian truffles that her grandmother taught her to make.

After heating up the candy mixture, I pour it onto a marble surface, a cutting board that my mom hardly uses. I wait until the candy cools and start forming balls that can be rolled into an assortment of sprinkles. Rolling each piece comes naturally, and it makes me feel better. Almost like yesterday never happened.

I find another serving dish. A festive one with red poinsettias painted on it. I place each candy on the plate so that they all line up perfectly. They are all the same size and the same chocolate flavor, but they alternate between chocolate sprinkles and Christmas sprinkles. I set the plate down on the counter and admire my work.

It was easy.

It was fun.

And I feel happier having accomplished their perfect circular shapes.

I take a large bite of an extra truffle that didn't fit onto the plate. It's still warm, and it's the right level of sweetness. I chew it slowly, thinking of all the times I've impatiently waited next to Grandma to take a first bite. Every year I would look forward to this.

The doorbell rings, and my brother and Lauren walk through the front door. My parents suggested that we all meet here and then choose a restaurant to go to. I pick up the tray of candies and grip it firmly as I walk into the living room. Mark spots me and watches me carefully, eyeing the tray as if I might drop it at any second.

"Don't worry," I joke. "I'm not going to drop it. I promise."

Lauren laughs a little to lighten the mood. She's carrying a couple gift boxes with red bows. She hands one to my mom, and then she hands one to me. I set the tray of Christmas sweets down on the coffee table and accept her gift. I don't know anything about Lauren, and my first impression of her wasn't exactly the greatest since she reminds me slightly of Georgina.

I neatly open her gift, making sure I smile as I do. I tear aside the wrapping paper and see a tiny, square canvas. A simple vanilla cupcake is painted on it. It has a baby blue wrapper with polka dots and a fondant pink heart on top. Lauren anxiously bites her lip and watches me observe the piece of artwork she selected.

"Wow," I mutter. "This will be perfect for my apartment."

"Oh, good. I'm glad you like it."

"I haven't really seen any cake art like this before." I study it again and gently touch the smooth paint strokes. Bree might try and steal this from me when we graduate. "Where did you get it? I might have to buy a couple more."

"Oh, I painted it myself." She clasps her hands together like it's no big deal.

"*You* painted this?"

"Lauren is an artist," Mark chimes in. "She works at a gallery in the city. That's how we met actually."

"I can paint you another if you'd like," she says.

"Really? I have a friend who would absolutely love one of these."

I wasn't sure about Lauren at first, but I guess I can learn to like her.

My mom grabs her coat and suggests a few places for dinner. All of which, as she puts it, have excellent vegetarian options. Dad chooses Italian and we all grab our coats and purses. Before we walk out the door I pick up the platter of Grandma's candies.

"Does anyone want one?" I look around. No takers. "Please. For old time's sake?"

"I'll try one," Lauren says. She steps forward first after nudging my brother to do the same.

"Okay," Mark agrees.

When Mark agrees my Mom takes a candy, and after she takes a bite my Dad grabs one too. All four of them nod as they slowly chew the sugary treat from our childhood. Lauren nods and reaches out to take another. Mom takes tiny bites, savoring each piece before she swallows it. I look at my dad twice, but I could have sworn that his eyes were misty for a brief second.

"I love them," Lauren comments.

"Yes honey, they are delicious," my mom adds.

"Just like Grandma's," Dad responds.

I take a deep breath, finally feeling as if I've succeeded in making everyone else as happy as I was when I made them. The atmosphere in the room feels different. Mom holds her smile for longer. Dad doesn't seem so distracted. Mark isn't clenching his jaw, and I'm not counting down the hours until I can fly back to school.

The lot of us are loosening up.

I set the tray down and pick up my jacket. My mom places her hand on my back as we step out into the gray winter air. She squeezes my shoulder and leans in to whisper something in my ear. They are the very words I was hoping to hear the moment I spotted her at baggage claim.

"Good job, honey. Good job."

CHAPTER TWENTY

I walk into our apartment back in Georgia and smell something burning. I wrinkle my nose, not used to this sort of thing because *Bree* is my roommate. She always says it's better to undercook something than it is to overcook something. I've never seen her burn a thing. *Never.*

"It's a sign from on high!" Bree shouts hysterically. "It's wrong. This is all wrong." She runs to the oven with a frown on her face and waves away a small cloud of smoke. She pulls a blackened pan out of the oven. I glance at it. My face twinges when I see rock hard brownies.

"It's okay." I attempt to calm her down but her face is flushed, and she looks like she might be wearing the same outfit she wore yesterday. And the day before that.

"It's not okay." She sits at the kitchen table and puts her head down. I glance at the pan, but none of the brownies are salvageable.

"So just try again," I suggest.

"I have." She sniffs and lifts her head only long enough to wipe her nose. "I've tried many, many times, but nothing ever works. I'm cursed. I should have never gone to that party during the break."

"Okay?" I say, unsure why she's having a meltdown over an overestimated baking time.

"I got my hair done," she goes on. "I bought a new dress. I made those mini cheesecakes that he likes so much."

"We are talking about *brownies* here?"

"I knew he had a thing for brunettes," she mutters. "But I didn't think he would bring one home to *marry*. I'm cursed. I have to be. I bet you anything some voodoo witch doctor cast a spell on me that time in college when my sorority sisters and I all went to New Orleans for Mardi Gras."

"Right," I improvise. "Because brownies and Louisiana can do all those things."

She finally takes a breath and looks up at me. She rubs her eyes, and I notice that her whole face looks ragged like she hasn't been able to sleep in days. I open the window in the kitchen to air out the smell and take a seat next to her.

"I take it your holiday wasn't pleasant?"

"My neighbor Todd," she responds. "I've had a crush on him since we were nine. He usually comes to my mom's Christmas party alone, but this time he brought a date." She rolls her eyes. "She had a ring on her finger the size of Texas."

"Ouch."

"Yeah." She glances at the pan of blackened brownies. "I need to get my mojo back if I'm going to have a chance at winning that contest."

Despite what Bree is going through, my heart leaps when she mentions the contest. I've been thinking of nothing else since I boarded my plane back to the South. I finally know what I'm going to do, and I have been practicing every chance I get.

I am going to make my grandma's candies. I don't care if they seem a little *too* simple. I don't think anyone can resist a beautiful box of gourmet truffles paired with roasted cocoa bean hot chocolate. Sometimes Grandma brewed cocoa beans the way she did coffee beans, and added a shot of the liquid to her hot chocolate for an extra kick. Like James said back in Alabama, it's a dessert that brings back all the good memories I have of my grandmother. To me that's a dish worth sharing.

"So have you locked down the red velvet layered cake?"

"Yeah." She nods. "That cake is my pride and joy." She pauses for a minute. "Dang. *That's* what I should have made for Todd this year."

"Don't worry about him, Bree. It's his loss."

"Maybe it won't last?" She shrugs. "What about you? Have you decided to enter a napoleon?"

"That was a bad idea the moment I thought of it," I admit. "No. I am going to make brigadeiro." She wrinkles her forehead. "They are handmade Brazilian truffles. My grandma's recipe."

Bree smiles.

"I bet they will taste amazing."

"As long as I beat Georgina," I reply.

"There's only one thing left to do then." She stands up and wipes at the makeup smearing under her eyes. "We need to go to the store for ingredients and get to work. The contest is next weekend."

"I can't wait for you to try one." I touch the wrinkled sleeve of her shirt. "But first, you could use a shower."

"Yeah," she responds, rubbing her eyes. "I've been a wreck ever since he introduced me to that tart."

"Wait here a second." I run to my room and dig out the cupcake painting from Lauren. Before she left she promised me that she would make me another one featuring a chocolate cupcake with rainbow sprinkles.

I return to the kitchen holding the painting, and Bree's eyes light up when she sees it. I was planning on giving her the chocolate one, but I know she would like either painting just the same. I hand it to her. Her eyes widen as she sits up and smiles, looking as if she might lick the frosting just to make sure it isn't real.

"Merry *belated* Christmas."

"Where did you get this?" she asks, astonished by the detail of each paint stroke.

"How much time do you have?"

She glances at her burnt brownies.

"If this involves girl talk you might want to hurry," she suggests. "Cole will be here any minute. I told him you were coming back today."

"Oh." My stomach fills with butterflies when she mentions his name. Other than a text message now and again, it has been a while since I've heard his voice.

Bree studies my expression. Her gaze meets mine, and I immediately look away. Bree giggles and heads towards the sink for a glass of water. She continues quietly laughing to herself as she fills a cup and opens the fridge to grab a leftover slice of lemon.

"Oh-my-gosh," she finally says. "You have a *thing* for Cole. I knew it."

"What makes you say that?"

"The look on your face," Bree answers.

"Am I not allowed to smile when you happen to mention his name?"

"It's not the smile. It's the way your entire face turns pink."

"It's a coincidence. It's hotter here than I'm used to."

"It always is, dear." She takes a sip of her lemon water and touches one of the mutilated brownies. She picks one up with a look of disgust on her face and then drops it back into the pan. It hits the surface with a loud thud.

"Hello?" There is a firm knock on the door. I answer it and feel a little flustered when I see Cole's face. I hesitate when my eyes fixate on his defined jawbone and fit torso. Bree is watching us more closely now.

"Hey," I respond. "How was your break?"

"Nothing exciting," he answers. "Except my cousin did bring an Auburn Tigers flag to dinner as a joke. That didn't go well. My uncle is a big Alabama fan." Cole spots the pan of burnt brownies and frowns. "What about you guys? Did anything interesting happen?"

Bree lightly hits her head against the table to avoid talking about her crush's fiancée. Detective Reid instructed my family to keep the incident with Dirk to ourselves, but I knew I wouldn't be able to keep the information in once I saw Bree and Cole again.

"You two better sit down," I say. I sit on the sofa in the living room and anxiously wait for them to join me.

"What happened?" Cole asks. "You seem a little…tense."

I discreetly glance at Bree. She grins and winks at me. I quickly move into my story about Dirk and the weed killer before Cole catches on. I don't want him to start asking questions and then feel uncomfortable because of Bree's awkward assumptions.

"Yeah, well, Detective Reid came to my house."

Cole leans forward in his seat.

"Why?" he asks.

"Okay," I sigh. "Maybe I should start from the beginning." I take a deep breath, wondering how they are going to react when I get to the part where I tossed food around like a lunatic until my mother started crying. "My parents threw their annual holiday party, only this time my mom had it catered, which was weird because she never does that." I look at Bree. "You were right. It was a special occasion. My brother proposed to his girlfriend."

"How wonderful," Bree responds. But her smile seems forced, and she grinds her teeth to keep herself from scowling. *Engagements* are the last thing she wants to hear about right now.

"Yeah, congratulations," Cole chimes in.

"Thanks. Anyway, I happened to be in the kitchen just before his big announcement, and I saw someone outside in the backyard, and…" This time I focus my attention on Cole because he went with me to Shurbin Farms. "I saw Dirk."

"Dirk?" Cole responds. "*Shurbin Farms* Dirk?"

"Uh-huh. Turns out he was the brains behind the operation this whole time."

"Ugh," Bree interjects. "I knew we were missing something."

"I guess Thomas Calle started smuggling stolen goods via the student bakery. He teamed up with some of the staff and made a fortune. But one night his father confronted him, they had an argument, and Thomas was kicked out."

"But he kept the business going," Bree finishes. "Impressive."

"So I guess James was lying when he told us that story about his Dad?" Cole clenches his fist.

"Not exactly," I answer. "James didn't know that Dirk's dad was Thomas' partner. Dirk took over when the two of them died, and he told me he was days away from retiring with all the cash."

"Wait a second." Cole clears his throat. "Dirk told you all that?"

"Yeah." I chuckle uncomfortably as my mind jumps back to me threatening him with a rock in the pouring rain. "He was definitely one to gloat."

"So what happened?" Bree urges me to continue.

"How the hell did he find out where you live?" Cole's jaw tightens as he narrows his eyes. He's angry that Dirk found me in the first place. "He must know where I live too."

"Don't worry," I reassure him. "He ran off, but Detective Reid's team is tracking him as we speak."

"So he says." Cole shakes his head.

"Let her finish," Bree cuts in.

"So Dirk told me all this stuff and then he ran off," I gulp. "And I looked in the trash can near where he was standing, and I found empty containers of weed killer."

"What a dick," she says boldly. She doesn't speak that way very often, but when she does I can't help but laugh.

"Bree," I scold her.

"What?" She throws her hands up in the air. "He spoiled all that good food just to get back at you. He deserves to be in jail."

"He tried to poison you?" Cole says, ignoring Bree completely. "*All* of you?"

"He tried, but I put a stop to it." I cough to clear my throat. This is the part that I've been dying to tell them. Mostly because my family refused to talk about it after Detective Reid left, and I feel like I need to let it all out of my system. "I sort of destroyed it all so no one would eat anything."

Cole and Bree look at each other.

"How?" Cole asks.

"I trashed every last dish," I confess. "I threw food on the floor, in the trash, everywhere really. No one would listen to me."

"You did all that?" Cole relaxes a little. He pauses, looking up a little as if he's trying to picture it.

"Yep."

Bree doesn't waste a minute. She begins laughing and covers her face when she can't seem to stop. Cole grins, and it makes me smile too. The way Bree wrinkles her nose when she laughs makes me chuckle. Before I know it, I join her. Cole watches me until the three of us are laughing together.

It feels good to be back at CPA.

* * *

I spent all night and morning making sure my entry looks exactly right. I want it to be a professional version of my grandma's homemade classic. Each truffle is exactly the same size, and the decorations are perfectly symmetrical. I picked out a sleek, brown chocolate box that looks like it could be found in a Parisian chocolate shop.

I enter the special event room that the school uses for dinners and receptions. Bree is at my side holding a cake box containing her red velvet cake with cream cheese frosting. The test cake that she baked tasted like heaven on a plate. The cake was moist and fluffy. It had that rich reddish color without all the food coloring. Her frosting was also spot-on. It was just the right texture and consistency, and most importantly it was not too sweet.

We are handed a number and an application to fill out. Bree and I snag presentation tables that are right next to each other and set down our desserts. I open my box of Grandma's brigadeiro and pull out a small glass mug. My thermos of hot chocolate is ready to be poured just before the judges approach my table. I look down at my creation. I enjoyed every minute I spent creating my dessert, and I think it shows.

I made six Brazilian truffles, and each one is a different flavor. There is a classic chocolate one rolled in chocolate jimmies. These are the ones Grandma Liz always made – the ones I made for my family over the holiday break. There is a vanilla truffle rolled in crystallized sugar. Next to it is a dark chocolate truffle rolled in crushed pistachios. The row below has my favorite one, the espresso-flavored truffle rolled in blue jimmies. Then there is the most colorful truffle. The Nutella truffle rolled in pink pearl sprinkles. And last is the truffle that I wish my grandma could have tried. I came up with a guava-flavored truffle rolled in coconut flakes.

I inhale the scent of my homemade hot chocolate with a shot of roasted cocoa beans for an extra kick. My entry is ready to be judged, and I am proud of it. I stand up taller and think of all the things I have accomplished here at CPA. I overcame being accused of stealing, becoming a possible murder suspect, and making some tragically dry piecrusts. I have come a *very* long way.

I feel a hand on my shoulder and turn around to see Cole. My chest tightens on its own when he looks at me. Cole studies my chocolate box pretending to size up his competition. I laugh as he scratches his chin.

"So what do you think?" I ask him.

"Those are definitely not napoleons," he responds.

"They are way better than plain old cream sitting on top of a stupid piece of dough." I gently touch the box as if it's a block of solid gold. "They are beautiful. They are rich and chocolaty, and they are going to win."

"Is that right, Lil' Mama?" He grins and takes a step closer. I can smell his cologne on his neatly pressed collared shirt.

"Don't act like you're not impressed." I smile and fidget with the hem of my charcoal colored blouse. I threw it on with a pair of skinny jeans and my black high-heeled boots, because it made my whole outfit look more conservative.

"Have you seen Georgina's..." He stops suddenly and stares at the front entrance. I turn around and see Jeff walk through the doors holding a plate of his sugar cookies with royal icing.

"I didn't think he would come," I comment. After the news spread about Mr. Harris, Jeff was sort of shunned by the rest of the class. No one talks to him much, and he keeps to himself. I do have to hand it to him for choosing to push through anyway until graduation. He must really want to open that bagel shop. "Excuse me for a second."

I walk up to him as he places his cookies on a table and clasps his hands together. He looks anxiously at his watch and then hides his hands in his pockets. His ice blue eyes widen when he sees me. I am still mad at him, but after what happened with Dirk, I've realized that life is too short to hold grudges.

"Poppy," he says quietly.

"Hey, Jeff," I respond. I look down at his entry, remembering the taste of it that I got at his apartment. The cookies look the same as they did back then, except Jeff made an extra effort to make the frosting look as smooth as possible. "I see you went with the sugar cookies. They look good, though that dessert bagel might have thrown a curveball at the judges."

"Thanks." He takes a breath almost like he's relieved that I'm not here to yell at him. "Look, Poppy, about all that stuff that happened—"

"Jeff." I hold up my hand. "I didn't come over here to tell you off. I actually wanted to say thank you."

"Really?"

"Yeah." I look down at my boots for a second. Half the school is watching us right now, and my cheeks are starting to feel hot. "You helped the police clear my name. I know it wasn't easy to tell the truth when it could've thrown your career down the toilet."

"I lucked out this time," he says quietly. "Mr. Dixon is going to let me stay and complete the program on the condition that I stay out of trouble, of course. And I have to work extra shifts at the bakery too."

"So you haven't been ordered not to speak to anyone," I tease.

"Everyone kind of does that on their own." He grins, looking a lot like his old self again.

"That will change. Pretty soon a new class of students will start their level one courses and everything will go back to normal."

"I hope you're right."

I nod and walk away just as Georgina walks past us and rolls her eyes. She tosses her blonde, curled hair over her shoulder and lifts her chin when she returns to her table. I glance at her entry and take a deep breath. I don't want her to know that I'm nervous that she might beat me.

Georgina is standing next to a tall croquembouche decorated with spun-sugar designs. I have seen pictures of these French desserts, but I've never actually made one or tasted one before. I assume that whoever wins the Paris internship will end up *croquembouche-ing* the day away. The dessert tower is cone-shaped. Each cream filled pastry ball is stacked perfectly on the next, and all of them are exactly the same shape. The tower is sitting on an elegant, crystal cake base, and the sugar designs are placed around the edges, mimicking a wedding cake. On top of the lovely French dessert is a delicate, chocolate sculpture.

I doubt she made this all on her own.

I have to hand it to Georgina. Her entry is a showstopper. I can already see the judges eyeing it, and it's not even time to begin the tastings. She glares at me as I pass her.

"Truffles," she teases. "*Really?*"

"Brazilian truffles," I correct her. I return to my table and wait for the judges to make an announcement. All of our displays are placed around the edges of the room, forming a circle. All of us have numbers, and in a few minutes the judges of the contest will circle around and taste everything. They will be carrying a clipboard with a scoring card. Once everything has been scored the students will then be free to circle around and taste each other's entries. During that time the scores will be tallied, and a winner will be named.

I made just enough candy to tempt the judges with Grandma's specialty.

I look across the room and see Cole nervously shifting from foot to foot. I smile when I see that he decided to make something that totally represents him. Butter rum bread pudding. He notices me looking at him, and the two of us make eye contact. He winks at me before looking away.

"Alright, students," Mr. Dixon says into a microphone. "It's time for the judges to make their rounds so make sure y'all are standing next to your entry, and be prepared to explain it to the judges."

I swallow the lump in my throat as I watch the judges begin at the first table—a girl in a different cooking group than mine who made a lemon meringue pie. The three judges examine her pie and cut a large slice of it.

"Did you see the other red velvet cakes?" Bree whispers. "There are three."

"Yours looks the best." I smile as I glance at her cake for the hundredth time. It's a modern version of an old-time classic.

The cake is sitting on a porcelain cake platter, and as Bree explained it, the cake is naked. That means that the sides of the cake are not frosted, so you can see the layers of cake and layers of frosting between. The top of the cake is decorated with a red fondant flower. I think the cake shows just how good she is with butter and sugar.

I tap my foot as the judges get closer and closer to me. When it is finally my turn I smile so widely that my face starts to hurt. I look at my brigadeiro and then look to see the expressions on their faces.

"Please explain your dessert," a man says with a French accent. I nod.

"This is brigadeiro with a cup of hot chocolate. I made six different flavors. There is a classic chocolate, vanilla, dark chocolate with pistachio, espresso, Nutella, and guava with coconut."

The man nods and places each truffle on a plate. He cuts them into pieces and takes a bite of the espresso one first. All three judges have blank expressions as they take notes. A student brings over a couple of sample cups so that the judges can try my hot chocolate. The French judge takes a sip and looks curiously at the glass mug.

"How did you make this?" he asks.

"Chocolate and steamed milk with a shot of roasted cocoa beans."

"You brewed cocoa beans like coffee?"

"Yes, I did," I reply, wondering if he meant that as an accusation or a compliment.

"Interesting," he mutters. He writes something down on his clipboard. "One more question. Why did you decide to make this?"

"Well, my grandma made it best," I begin. "But I suppose I wanted to present you with something that represents me as a chef. My greatest hope is that you'll bite into one of these Brazilian truffles and find yourself being transported to an old woman's kitchen in a tiny little village where they don't own mixers or piping bags or convection ovens."

"Would you say that the old way of doing things is best?" the man asks. I bite the side of my lip and hope that he's not trying to trick me into looking stupid.

"I think the modern kitchen shouldn't completely discard the past," I answer. The old man nods, and I can see a twinkle in his eye like he's trying to hold in a grin.

The judges move on to Bree's cake. I watch them cut a slice and examine the layers of cake and frosting throughout the dessert. The French judge digs a fork into it first. He chews with precision, looking up as he does as if he is scoring the cake in his head. I hear him ask Bree the same question he asked me. "Why did you decide to make a red velvet cake?"

Bree mentions that the recipe has been in her family for a long time. I see her look over at the other red velvet entries. She quickly adds that her recipe is made with natural red coloring. The judges nod and move to the next table.

When the judging is over, I hesitate to move around the room and taste the competition. I can barely focus as I check the time every other minute. I *really* want to win that internship with Jean Pierre. If I don't win then I'll settle for Bree or Cole winning the prize.

"Nothing left," a voice says beside me. I turn around and look into the face of Detective Reid. "I hope that means it was good?"

"Detective," I respond. His presence is such a surprise that my chest starts pounding out of control. I clear my throat and brace myself for bad news. He always seems to come bearing bad news. "I didn't think I would hear from you again so soon."

"I wanted to see you in person." He nods and casually looks around. "We apprehended Dirk trying to cross the border into Canada."

"I can finally sleep easy," I respond.

"Yes, you can." He glances around the room with his hands in his pockets. I guess now that I'm not a murder suspect or a possible victim anymore, he doesn't know what to say to me. He looks over at Bree's red velvet cake. "Impressive. I can barely microwave popcorn."

"So." I change the subject to something he is more familiar with. "Did you recover all the missing black truffles?"

"Most of them." He sighs. "I'll tell you though. I can't believe that whole operation was running on campus for so long without anybody noticing. Either you're a brilliant spy or you are attracted to trouble."

"Well, I doubt anything that crazy will ever happen to me again."

"You never know," he says lowly.

"Attention students," Mr. Dixon announces. The room falls silent. "I would like to introduce you to Mr. Jean Pierre's assistant and the general manager of Le Croissant, Michel Rolph." The French judge walks to the microphone and smiles as all the students clap.

"Merci," he responds. "All of you have presented very impressive and very refined desserts. I am looking for a very specific chef to take part in our internship at Le Croissant. This student must be skilled, organized, diligent, and most importantly, in love with learning." Michel hands the microphone back to Mr. Dixon.

"Thank you, Mr. Rolph," he says. He looks down at his paper and pauses. "This was a close one folks. The runner-up if our winner is not able to complete the internship's prerequisites goes to Georgina Levens!"

Georgina claps uncomfortably as she looks around at her classmates with a fake smile. The expression on her face is worth all the trouble I went through this year to stay at Calle Pastry Academy. Georgina takes a few steps towards Mr. Dixon, but she stops when she realizes that there is nothing for the second place student to receive but a pat on the back. No certificate. No plaque. No prize money. Not even a bouquet of flowers. I cover my mouth with my hand, trying not to laugh too loud.

"And our *winner* is..." Mr. Dixon pauses again. My stomach churns, and I feel Bree squeeze my arm. "Well, what do you know—our winner is Ms. Poppy Peters!" The entire room breaks out in cheers and clapping. I am so shocked that I can't move. Bree nudges my shoulder.

I am going to Paris.

Georgina turns around and looks at me.

"Congrats, Poppy," Georgina says with a smirk on her face. "I was just in Paris last fall, so I'm good."

"So glad you're such a good sport," I sarcastically respond.

"Clearly the judges were looking for something more…" She glances at my empty chocolate box. "Homely."

I keep a smile on my face, but inside I am screaming at her.

Total brat!

"Whatever," I mutter. She raises her eyebrows and places her hands on her hips. I find it comical that she's wearing beige slacks and a white blouse at a dessert competition. I'm surprised her shirt doesn't have any stains on it yet.

"Good luck," she laughs. "After what happened to the last intern, I didn't really want that position anyway."

I glare at her as she strides away to admire her croquembouche some more. Cole walks right up to me and gives me a hug. I inhale his cologne and feel his muscles tighten around me. My cheeks feel warm, and I want to break away, but I like hugging him.

"I can't believe this, Poppy." Bree interrupts us. Cole and I both pull away from each other at the same time.

"I know," I admit. "Paris!"

"Promise me you'll still take that wedding cake class with me," Bree pleads.

"Of course," I agree. I glimpse down at my boots, dwelling on Georgina's words. "Hey, you don't happen to know what happened to the last Paris intern, do you?"

"Oh," Cole responds. "So that's what Georgina told you. Don't worry about it, Poppy. You are going to have a kick-ass time in Paris."

"Cole," I scold him. "Details. Now."

"Um." Cole's eyes dart around the room.

"Cole."

"Fine," he sighs. "He came home early. I guess he went a little crazy because he couldn't handle the pressure. *You* will be fine though. I know you will."

"I always am," I reply.

RECIPES

——

SOUTHERN PEACH PIE

———

CRUST
3 cups all-purpose flour
1 teaspoon salt
1 cup cold unsalted butter (2 sticks)
3/4 cup half-and-half

FILLING
6-8 ripe peaches
1/2 - 3/4 cup vanilla sugar (can substitute with regular granulated sugar or homemade brown sugar with spices)
1 tablespoon freshly squeezed lemon juice
1/4 cup flour
1-2 tablespoons unsalted butter

For the crust, combine the flour and the salt in a large bowl. Cut the cold butter into 1-inch cubes and add to the flour mixture. Blend the flour mixture and butter together in a food processor until butter pea-sized or use a bowl, and cut the butter with a fork into the mixture until it resembles coarse meal. Add the half-and-half, and stir the mixture with a fork until all the flour is moistened. Shape the dough into a ball using your hands. Cover the dough with plastic wrap, and refrigerate while you make the pie filling (30 minutes to an hour).

For the filling, peel off the skins and slice the peaches into 3/4 inch thick slices. Mix together the peaches, lemon juice, flour, and vanilla sugar in a large bowl. Start with 1/2 cup of sugar and add more if desired.

Split the dough into two balls. For the bottom crust, roll the dough to about an 1/8 inch thickness on a floured surface. Transfer to the pie pan, making sure the dough hangs over the edges of the pan. Add the peach filling. Cut 1-2 tablespoons of unsalted butter into slices and scatter on top of the peach filling. Roll the second half of the dough to about an 1/8 inch thickness on a floured surface and place over the peach filling. Pinch the edges of the bottom layer of dough into the top layer of dough and trim any excess on the edges. Make sure the edges of the pie are tightly sealed. Cut a few slits into the top crust to allow steam to escape. Brush the top crust with milk and sprinkle it with about 1 teaspoon of sugar.

Place a baking sheet in the oven underneath the pie to catch any drips. Bake at 375 degrees Fahrenheit for 45-60 minutes, until the filling is bubbling and the crust is golden brown. If the crust browns too quickly, cover the pie with foil to prevent the crust from burning or getting too dark.

Optional Lattice Pattern:
To create a lattice pattern with the top crust, roll the dough on a floured surface and use a pizza cutter or sharp knife to cut into even strips. Make them as wide or as thin as desired as long as they are all the same width. Also, make sure that the bottom crust is long enough to hang over the edges of the pan. Add the peach filling on top of the bottom layer of crust. Lay half the strips horizontally over the pie spaced evenly, making sure that the edges of each strip are long enough to reach the edges of the pan. Fold every other strip back on itself. Lay one of the remaining strips of dough vertically across the center of the pie so that it lies across the unfolded horizontal strips, not the folded pieces. Unfold the folded pieces so that they lay on top of the vertical strip. Fold the strips of dough that have not been folded and add another vertical strip across the pie. Continue swapping the folded and unfolded horizontal strips, adding another vertical strip each time until half of the pie is latticed. Continue this pattern with the other half of the pie until the entire pie is latticed. Crimp and trim the edges. Brush the top crust with milk and sprinkle with about 1 teaspoon of sugar. Bake as normal.

VANILLA SUGAR

—————

1 vanilla bean
2 cups granulated sugar
1 air-tight container or Mason jar

Quick Method:
Cut the vanilla bean down the middle, and use a knife to scrape
out the center. Add scrapings to a container or Mason jar of
sugar. Rub the scrapings into the sugar by hand until the vanilla
is evenly distributed throughout the container. Seal and set aside.
This sugar can be used right away if needed. The vanilla will age
over time, becoming more fragrant and gradually giving the
sugar a stronger vanilla taste.

Aged Vanilla Sugar:
To make aged vanilla sugar you can use a new vanilla bean or
one that has already been used in a previous recipe. If you are re-
using a vanilla bean that has already been cooked it must be air
dried first. Place the bean in a container of sugar, and cover the
bean with sugar. Seal the container or Mason jar and set aside. In
2-3 weeks the vanilla bean will have infused with the sugar.
More vanilla beans can be added for a stronger taste and
fragrance. Over time the sugar will become lightly brown in
color.

Gift Ideas:
Both of these methods can also be used with pink sugar crystals.
Seal the sugar in a decorative jar to give as a gift or party favor.
To create a homemade sugar scrub, add 1 part oil to 2 parts sugar
(1/2 cup oil for 1 cup sugar). Recommended oils are olive oil,
almond oil (or any nut oil), or coconut oil. Add 1/2 teaspoon
Vitamin E oil. Add several drops of lemon, orange, or lavender
essential oil (optional). Mix together and seal in an airtight
container. The sugar scrub will last up to 2 months.

HOMEMADE BROWN SUGAR WITH SPICES

---

2 tablespoons molasses
1 cup granulated sugar
1/4 teaspoon of one or more of the following spices (optional):
ginger, allspice, cloves, cinnamon, nutmeg

In a bowl, vigorously mix together the sugar and molasses using a fork. Add more molasses to make darker brown sugar, and add more granulated sugar to create a lighter brown sugar. Mix in the spices for additional flavor (optional). Use right away or store in an airtight container or Mason jar.

Gift Ideas:
Seal the sugar in a decorative jar to give as a gift or party favor. To create a homemade sugar scrub, add 1 part oil to 2 parts sugar (1/2 cup oil for 1 cup sugar). Recommended oils are olive oil, almond oil (or any nut oil), or coconut oil. Add 1/2 teaspoon Vitamin E oil. Mix together and seal in an airtight container. The sugar scrub will last up to 2 months.

BUZZ'S RISE & SHINE ORANGE ROLLS

DOUGH
5 1/2 - 6 cups all-purpose flour
2 teaspoons salt
1 egg, beaten
2 cups warm water
2 tablespoons yeast
1/3 cup sugar
1/3 cup vegetable oil

FILLING
1/2 cup (1 stick) unsalted butter, softened
1/2 cup sugar
1 tablespoon grated orange rind

ORANGE GLAZE
2 cups powdered sugar
1/4 cup orange juice (freshly squeezed without pulp is preferable)
1 teaspoon vanilla extract

For the dough, combine the yeast, sugar, and oil in a large mixing bowl. Add the warm water. The yeast should start to foam in 5-10 minutes. Add the beaten egg and stir well. Add the salt with the flour, mixing in one cup of flour at a time until the dough is workable. Knead for 1-2 minutes, cover with a towel, and let the dough rise for about an hour or until the dough has doubled in size. Split the dough into two equal pieces.

For the filling, mix together the softened butter, sugar, and orange rind so that the mixture is spreadable. Roll the dough on a floured surface into a rectangular shape (about 8 x 12 inches) and spread the butter mixture on top. Roll each portion of the dough jelly roll-style, as you would with cinnamon rolls. Seal and pinch the seams, and cut into thick slices (about 1/2 inch). Place the slices on a greased baking pan or in a casserole dish, cover, and let the rolls rest and rise for about an hour.

Bake at 350 degrees Fahrenheit for 15-20 minutes or until the rolls are lightly browned.

To make the glaze, sift the powdered sugar and combine with the orange juice and vanilla extract. Mix well. Drizzle over the warm rolls after they come out of the oven.

STUDENT UNION BLUEBERRY SCONES

———

2 cups all-purpose flour
1/2 cup sugar
2 teaspoons baking powder
1/4 teaspoon salt
1/2 teaspoon cinnamon
1/2 teaspoon cardamom (optional)
6 tablespoons cold unsalted butter
1 cup heavy cream
1 cup fresh blueberries

Mix together the flour, sugar, baking powder, salt, cinnamon, and cardamom (optional). Cut the butter into small cubes and blend with flour mixture in a food processor. (If you do not have a food processor, rub the butter into the flour mixture with your fingertips until it resembles coarse meal.) Add the heavy cream, and blueberries. Mix together and form a circle of dough about 8 inches in diameter and 1 ½ inches thick on a floured surface. Cut the dough into 8 wedges and place them on a baking sheet. Brush the tops with milk (or beaten egg) and sprinkle with sugar. Bake at 375 degrees Fahrenheit for 20-25 minutes until golden brown.

BLACK MARKET BEIGNETS

———

4 cups all-purpose flour
3 teaspoons yeast
1/4 cup homemade brown sugar (substitute regular sugar if desired)
1/2 teaspoon salt
1/2 cup evaporated milk
1 egg
2 tablespoons unsalted butter, softened
1 cup warm water
2-3 cups powdered sugar, for dusting
Oil, for frying

In a large bowl, mix together the flour, sugar, salt, evaporated milk, and yeast. Add the warm water. Mix in the beaten egg and softened butter. Cover and let the dough rise for about an hour. Roll the dough on a floured surface until it is about 1/2 inch thick, and cut into squares. In a pot or deep pan, use enough oil to fully submerge the dough, but make sure the pan is less than half way full. Heat the oil to 365 degrees Fahrenheit, and fry the beignets for 2-3 minutes until golden brown. Let them cool and sprinkle with powdered sugar. Makes about 2 dozen.

VEGAN CHOCOLATE CAKE

CAKE
2 1/4 cups all-purpose flour
1/2 cup cocoa powder
1 1/2 cups granulated sugar
1 teaspoon baking soda
1/4 teaspoon baking powder
1/2 teaspoon salt
1 cup warm water or coffee
1/2 cup vegetable oil
2 teaspoons vanilla extract

DARK CHOCOLATE GANACHE
1/2 cup coconut milk
4-5 ounces dark chocolate

For the cake, mix together the flour, cocoa powder, sugar, salt, baking soda, and baking powder in a large bowl. In a separate bowl, combine the vegetable oil, vanilla, and water or coffee. Slowly add the wet ingredients to the dry mixture. Pour the batter into a greased, 9-inch Bundt pan, baking dish, or cake pan. Bake at 350 degrees Fahrenheit for 30-35 minutes until a toothpick comes out clean.

Prepare the ganache by melting together the dark chocolate and coconut milk in a saucepan or the microwave. The ganache should be thin enough to pour across the top of the cake. Remove the cake from the pan and drizzle over the warm cake, and let it all cool before serving.

BREE'S RED VELVET CAKE

CAKE
2 1/2 cups all-purpose flour
1 1/2 cups granulated sugar
1 teaspoon baking soda
1 teaspoon salt
2 tablespoons cocoa powder
1/2 vegetable oil
3/4 cup milk
1/2 cup beet puree (See instructions below)
2 eggs
2 tablespoons red food coloring (optional if a redder color is preferred)
1 teaspoon vanilla extract
1 teaspoon apple cider vinegar

CREAM CHEESE FROSTING
16 ounces cream cheese
1/2 cup unsalted butter (1 stick)
1 teaspoon vanilla extract
2 cups white chocolate chips, melted
2 cups powdered sugar, sifted

For the cake, mix together the flour, sugar, salt, and cocoa powder in a large mixing bowl. In a separate bowl mix together the vegetable oil, milk, beet puree, eggs, vanilla extract, and red food coloring. In a third bowl, combine the baking soda with the apple cider vinegar. After it foams, add it to the bowl of wet ingredients. Slowly mix the wet ingredients into the dry mixture. Pour the batter into a greased, 9-inch cake pan. Bake at 350 degrees Fahrenheit for 30-35 minutes, until a toothpick inserted into the center of the cake comes out clean.

For the frosting, beat together the cream cheese, butter, and vanilla extract. Add the melted white chocolate, and then slowly mix in the powdered sugar. Frost the cake after it has been removed from the pan, and has had time to cool.

For beet puree:
Boil 3-4 beets in water for about 30 minutes until the beets are easily pierced with a fork. Rinse and let them cool, keeping the water used to boil them. When the beets have cooled, remove the skin (should come off easily) and roughly chop. Use a food processor or blender to pulse the beets until smooth, using the leftover water to achieve a smooth consistency.

Alternatively, you can also puree a (15 oz) can of sliced beets. One can will make about a cup of puree.

COLE'S AUNT'S EASY ÉCLAIR PIE

---

2 small (1 oz) packages French vanilla pudding
8 ounces Cool Whip
1 (14.4 oz) box graham crackers
4 tablespoons unsalted butter
4 tablespoons milk
4 tablespoons unsweetened cocoa powder
2 cups powdered sugar

Prepare the French vanilla pudding as per instructions, and fold
in Cool Whip. Line the bottom of a 9x13 casserole dish with
graham crackers. Pour half the pudding mixture on top, add
another layer of graham crackers, and pour the rest of the
pudding over it. Add a final layer of graham crackers. Melt
together the butter, milk, and cocoa powder. Remove from heat
and slowly whisk in the powdered sugar. Pour the chocolate
sauce onto the top layer of graham crackers. Serve right away or
place in the fridge overnight. Save any excess chocolate to serve
on the side.

GRANDMA'S PRIZE WINNING BRIGADEIRO

---

2 tablespoons unsalted butter
2 (14 oz) cans sweetened condensed milk
1-2 tablespoons unsweetened cocoa powder
Chocolate sprinkles for decorating

First, prepare a smooth surface to let the candy cool. You can use a smooth countertop, cutting board, or baking sheet. The candy mixture will need to be mixed quickly and poured to cool to prevent it from burning. In a medium saucepan, melt the butter on medium to high heat. Add the sweetened condensed milk and cocoa powder, and turn the heat to high. Mix quickly with a metal spoon until the mixture starts to bubble. You will know the candy is ready to pour onto a cool surface when the mixture starts to pull away from the sides of the pan on its own. Pour the mixture onto prepared surface, and let it cool until it is warm (about 30-60 minutes). When it is cool enough to touch, pull away pieces and begin rolling the candy into even size balls. Roll the balls in a bowl of chocolate sprinkles until the entire surface is covered. If the mixture is too sticky to do this, then it needs to cool a little longer.

ABOUT THE AUTHOR

A. Gardner is a native westerner exploring the sweet bites of the south. After years of working in the healthcare industry, she moved across the country with her husband and adventurous baby boy. She is a mystery and romance writer with a serious cupcake obsession and a love of storytelling that began at an early age. When she is not writing, she is either chasing after her son, out for a swim, trying out a new recipe, or painting her nails bright blue.

To learn more about A. Gardner, visit her online at:
http://www.gardnerbooks.blogspot.com

Enjoyed this book? Check out these other novels available in print now from Gemma Halliday Publishing:

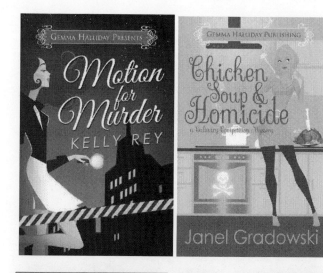

www.GemmaHallidayPublishing.com

Made in the USA
Charleston, SC
16 March 2015